BLOCK LEGEND PAPER
BY THE TON V

KEVIN GREEN

authorHOUSE®

AuthorHouse™
1663 Liberty Drive
Bloomington, IN 47403
www.authorhouse.com
Phone: 833-262-8899

Published by AuthorHouse 11/11/2020

ISBN: 978-1-6655-0777-6 (sc)
ISBN: 978-1-6655-0776-9 (e)

BURNING FLAME

REWRITE **

Watching the campfire feeling the heat of the flames, watching the glow change shape as the colors intertwine, from white, to blue to red, eating the wood alive, listening to the snaps and crackles that seem to jump at me, mesmerising me putting me in a trance, a state of clamness and please watching the fire change face, shape and color, telling the stories of life and with the right eye, even telling stories of the future to come in the distance, giving off life, and warmth for those close, providing safety for those who remain close to the flames but never to close, the fire can provide life to those who learn to control it, lessening the chance of danger, and providing light for the night, giving and taking all it can while the flames still burn eating the wood alive while the flames transform forever changing shape, to fit the situation changing for different reasons burning wood from different seasons, while I watch the stories of the flames transform, mesmerized by the heat and color of the flames burning as bright as the night will allow, watching the flames reach out and touch those who remain to close to the heat, I can feel my face warming up, I can see the glow from the fire reflecting on my skin, watching the flames wondering if it's the same heat that lies within, feeling the warmth of the fire coat my skin, somehow fueling the life that burns within. Listening to the fire talk wondering how to talk back, watching the sparks from the fire jump from the front to back, burning out in the cool night air, loosing the energy to live on, while the fire lives on burning as strong as ever before, sitting by the campfire watching the fire live on. Watching the stories of life change within the flames as the fire constantly changes with every gust of wind, feeling the warmth of the fire coat my skin. Danger is always possible when dealing with heat, so I must watch my step and remain cautious, so I don't get burned, watching the fire so dangerous and mysterious change tempeture and shape eating the firewood, letting smoke fill the air, soaking in the stories of the flames, watching the fire light up the night sky sending smoke signals to those above, listening to the fire for life's answers listening to the stories that the fire has to tell, soaking up the warmth from the flame and that warming campfire smell, as the flames change and rearrange changing with the beat of life, watching the fire light up the night as the fire glow over so bright, as the fire teaches those the rules of the flames as the color of the flames change shape, always ready to consum life mesmerized by the glow, watching the fire change from blue to red hot to the color of the purest white snow, keeping a safe distance from the heat of the fires burning glow, as the fire changes with the wind, rearranging as the time passes, mesmerized by the glow as time passes on.

*

Back up on the block again remembering the good times and hard crimes out here roaming the street one hand steady stuck to the wheel with the unknown nine posted laying low kicking back chilling waiting up under the seat out here staying stuck to the grind out here with a price you can't beat windows tinted incase niggas gotta try to turn up the heat back up on the block again steady smoking hustle on rising to the top again making the wheels spin remembering how these nigga cold cocked a nigga and split a niggas frame hard it all until the fall watching these niggas started throwing salt in the game trying to take the eye of the tiger from a nigga but I'm a beast that can't be tamed these niggas don't deserve to win if these don't play by the rules and regulation of the game do the crime do the crime and never ever roll over I know these niggas play for keep I'm a motherfucking street soldier on the hunt for the motherfucka that crossed the line and tried to take the game over I'm a nigga that don't like to move over back to the block to take the game back and push these niggas motherfucking heads over I already reached the bottom sticking to the rules and regulation because those niggas hating, sitting back low key me and my nina waiting my nigga I'm on the rise to the top out here roaming the hood I can't wait to find yo spot listening to my lovely nina nine cockback the only the to rise to the top is to take my respect ride by the block and take back my spot I know these niggas know me and for some strange motherfucking reason they don't think they owe me keep yo ears open and mouth closed and soak the game up that's what a wise man told me back up on the block again to take back what these motherfuckas owe me eyies on the prize out to get my money power and my motherfucka respect nina loaded up and ready to blow when I catch up with these nigga I'm a make sure they give me what I came for in times of war you should keep yo nina on yo lap at all times these motherfucka catching the whole clip plus one when I come to take mine searching for a spot I can't wait to find out here niggas play for keeps nigga I'm here to take mine

The maddness that creapt inside my home the lights continue to dim as I watch the rains fall trying to fight the whispers that have put an end to it all. I put an end to the whispers and the whispers put an end to it all lights off the rain stops and that's all no more whispers no more voices and no more strain, no more pain at all

spitting white fire out of the barrel of the beast locked and ready to release heat kick a nigga head back and sweap his ass off his feet no need to get up nigga, leave you leaking in your seat I'm blazing and I stay hotter then I'm suppose to, no time to argue nigga I protect mine with my tech nine like I'm suppose too don't test my nuts I'll push a nigga head back just to watch his head snap and crack open I know this nigga can't keep talking with that hole wide open close a niggas mouth piece while my gun still smoking I told you pussy nigga I'm hot got a bullet with your name on it ready and willing to find the right spot don't fuck with me nigga unless you want to fuck me nigga I'm standing here itching to use my trigger finger no need to talk shit when I can put my finger in your hole don't fuck with me nigga I'm hot and my nuts on side

Whispers awaken me from sleep, voices I can't see taunt me taken time away from sleep taring at my mental state voices that don't know me, unsure of the area of pain that needs to beat out or release from me haunted by the voices that have awaken me, continously taunting me driving a sane man insane searching for the insane parts as I pick through my brain watching the red rain as I search through with persition watching the red rain as the pain continues to blur my vision taunted by voices I can't see but I can hear with the cleanest clearity trying to find a way to deafen the voices the continuously continue to haunt me, these noises are driving me up the wall cutting away at the maddness watching the red rain fall fighting the whispers that have awaken me fighting the inner demons where has this maddness taken me or maybe this is the maddness that is making me mad or maybe the voices that taunt me are voices I never had forgetting if it's the voices or the red rain that makes me insane feeling the warmth of the flow of red rain and the truest feeling of pain trying to find the problems of life that continue to enter my brain. The whispers have awaken me so close and yet so distance I feel so far away from home cutting at the maddness that torments me watching the rain fall while I search through the bone accompanyed by the feeling of pain and the release of endorfins watching my body twich as I feel the rush of pain enter and travel up my spin searching for this insanity of mine I know I can find it every search takes time trying my best to deafen the whispers that haunt me turn down the volume of the voices that taunt me watching the rain fall I can trust the pain, the pain is real but these voices of insanity are driving me insane pealing away the skin trying to release the pressure from my brain trying to remain calm through every rush and jolt of pain accompanied by the rain, the rain that never stops searching for the whispers that haunt me hoping for the maddness to stop. Remembering when life had a purpose holding a flap of skin trying my best to stay in focused trying to cut away the pain that causes havoc on my brain it's easier to live with physical pain then the stress and strain of this insanity that rotts my brain, searching to find the maddness that's eating me alive cutting away layer after layer of matter hoping I'm doing fine. I can't seem to stop the pain no matter how far I dig they continue to defeat me, wondering how can whispers I can't see continue to beat me these voices are eating me alive I'm trying to cut away the maddness I think I'm doing fine watching the rain fall accompanied by this pain of mine these voices in my head are harder to get rid of then the bone, I can live with the pain but the mental strain won't leave me alone searching for these voices as I start to cut through the bone trying to cut away the maddness that has entered my home how can a totally sane man turn insane tormented by voices he can't see I'm dying to find out trying my best to cut this maddness out of me don't know how to rid myself of this mental strain trying to cut out the maddness, the whispers that lie deep within the brain holding my skull in place as I continue to pick my brain wondering if it's just me or could it be the voices in my head trying to cut away the insanity, rid myself of this grief and torment the pain that lies inside trying to cut away the maddness that by brain tries to hide hoping to ease the pain as I watch the rain fall watching the lights dim as I start to loose focus cutting away the maddness now the whispers start to deafen and the voices start to drift away I cut deep enough to deafen the whrispers but now the rain won't go away feeling the light go dark looking at my reflexion of two shades where have I gone there's nothing but insanity now the sane man's gone trying to cut away

*MORE SEX, MORE VIOLENCE, MORE DETAILS, MORE DEPTH, VISUAL THOUGHTS MORE STORIES TO REMEMBER, MORE CHARACTER TO THE CHARACTERS

+ Outline
+ Story (plot)
+ Characters
+ Beinging, middle and ending
+ depth to scenes, and characters
+ Great dialogue

+Misconception of freedom, everything in this country can be bought, there is no freedom here only money, and power you can even buy respect, the weight is for the man at the bottom of the tottom pole, the only way to win is to spend if you want to live the high life you have to pay the price and life ain't cheap up here, we do thing that people dream about doing every day, we buy this, we pay for that money in one pocket and out the other, we can't have people walking away with the money we rightfully earned. The money we spill tears, sweet, and blood over, we have to cut the head off the snake before it bites, not after we've been bitten. That's the way we have to play the game, the rules and regulation have to be follow exactly as plan in order for things to flow as smooth as they do, I wouldn't be telling this, if it wasn't true. If we don't stop it now, they will nickle and dime us to death, and I don't know about you but I love my life, this drink couldn't taste better, life is always sweater when you have something to live for. Our job is to strike while the iron's hot, and to keep the fire hot enough to cook anything that comes our way, that's the price we pay for living the life we live, there is no freedom here only money, and power. + If it wasn't for us things around here would fall apart, we clean up the mess after the shit hits the fan and I can always smell it, bullshit still smells like bullshit, no matter what you do with it, it's still shit.

+ Right now I'm just holding on to life, and I can't control which direction, stuck in all this bullshit while everything we built is starting to fall apart and turn to shit, we spent too much time and money, too much blood sweat and tears to see everything fall apart in our hands

+ living the life with no strings attached it seems like everything is all down hill from here, life couldn't get any better.

+ After running around for the day, I stayed home sometimes life just seems better that way, give myself time to wash off some of the stress that's builds up on the shoulders I like to stay clean.

+ If your too nice, these people will walk right over you, and won't look back, keep business, business even when it's personal

This was the life I always dreamed about, belonging to a group of high society sociallites with the pull and power to make anything happen and to make trouble disaper forever. Where everyone had money to spend, where the money rolled in and never stops, a place where dreams came true, ever better then I could imagine, and sometimes better then my dreams, this was the life, nothing like the day in the car, that day seemed to just drift away, further and further away everyday, sometimes I looked back and almost forgot that it happened, but in reality I know it did, the first time my soul was stained with the blood of someone else. That day seemed worlds away from where my life was, and even further away from where my life was going. Everything was getting bigger and brighter for me and the inner circle, it felt like things could get no better. The money was rolling in, it was like everything sold itself like we had the market on automatic, while we sat back and watch the money rollin, it was the life, like ice cold lemonade on a hot summers day, making money with the inner circle just felt like the perfect situation, money to spend, money to save and money to burn, I could wipe my ass with a wodd of money and flush it down the toilet and it wouldn't have mattered. I would have made it all back plus some in only a few hours without doing a thing, things were running that smooth, within the inner circle it felt like I couldn't loose and nothing could stop the money or the flow of merchindice. We had it on lock and we were the only ones with the key, and the local police knew all about it, when something happen they just turned their backs and let it slide as long as they got their cut it didn't matter, and if something went wrong with our plans we always had the chief of police to protect the circle, he would give a member of the circle a call to warn us of anything that was out of the ordinary protecting themselves of course, and the inner circle at all times, people on our team making drops left and right, shipments coming in it seemed like twenty four hours a day. Sometimes I had to ask what day it was two or three times a day, I've barly had time to sleep and when we did sleep it was usually between a drop off between parties or before or after business meetings. It seemed like every time I sat down I had to get back up to make sure this shipment got to this location, this shipment made it to this location, making sure everything was how it was suppose to be, and most importantly no problems with the product, the inner circle always had to keep up the reputation of having the best, being the best, that's how we controled the market. <u>Everyone got their cuts</u> without arguements or scuffles or problems of any nature, everyone was kept happy, because everyone was a part of the inner circle, and if you were a part of the inner circle you were family.

(I need to handle some unfinish business (extinguisher) (I be back), I'll see you tomorrow)

+ Took one last ride with his close friend someone he highly respected cracked a few jokes and as soon as he got out of the car he picked his loaded gun up, turned the safety off and blew his brains all over the window (Sorry, you had to pay what you owe, I told him not to cross me, I told him, why didn't he listen, I told him, exactly what the rules were and he broke the number one rule don't steal and <u>don't bit the hand that feeds you</u> I told and now it's nothing I can do,) as he pulls the lifeless body from the car before he gets rid of the evidence and and takes the body to the hospital garage and waits until it safe to bring the body into the morge and toe tag it filling out all the nessasary paperwork leaving no trace of the matter except for a dead body and an evidence trail that led to nowhere. It was something he always hated to do, but somebody had to clean up the mess and take care of business no matter what and this mess had be cleaned before the problem got to big at handle, or just out of control.

Later on, way later on Ending if I find a better ending then I'll replace shit the ups and downs. I guess it's true what they say life don't fail

• They cut the legs from under me, my connect disowned me, circle, my clientel was stolen, my jewelery, diamonds was stolen, knocked out of the party, got me kicked out of my house, kicked out of the state they broke in and stole everything I need and left me with nothing. They only thing left was my life and the game the streets gave me. I had no choice but to leave and start over again. Nerver thought I'd have to run with my tail between my legs. How did it go wrong? How did the tables turn against me, everything was everything until everything was gone. I had to leave before my life was taken and even though I left before they took my life I still felt, somebody was watching me. Shit as long as I'm still alive I won't be down for long payback a motherfucka ain't it.

• I guess the reason they left me alive, because the money didn't stop just the playas in the game change, and they know they knew too much about me and I'm no snitch, I never broke any of the rules or regulations to the game, I guess I should have known better it was too good to be true, I'm good at what I do I know I would be down for long, I was taught to be the best, I just have to start over, and play the game according to the rules and regulations to the game. I won't be down for long. Never matter what I won't be able to forget what I learned and all the people I met, now it's all up hill and all I have to do is make it to the top, just me, my balls and my word. You win some you lose so, but I know I'll make it to the top again. I always do all I gotta do is play smart, stick to the rules and regulation of the game and take it one step at a time I won't be down for long.

•I met this beautiful woman at one of the inner circle parties, her name was _____, I was introduced by _____, she showed me around the house, the place was built like a palace, all sorts of exspensive things indoor outdoor pool with a indoor jacuse and sauna, water fountains outside, they even had a few fountains inside, gamerooms, wine cellar, I couldn't count the number of balconies, bedrooms, and bathrooms, a garage that could hold a small car lot with all types of brand new exspensive vehicals and other pricey things, she showed me all around the grounds of the _____ home. And after I got an eye full she took me to the bedroom and closed and locked the door and after we were finished she gave me a smile told me she'd be back, and the next thing I knew, I was getting taken advantage of by her and her friend I didn't know, we were never introduced, and once she got her fill she left us alone to finish up. When she left she gave me a smile and closed the door behind her and locked it on her way out. I was having the time of my life and none of it was suspected, but I hold no problems at all staying up for the challenge. I don't need to say it, but it was I night worth remembering. I never did catch _____ friends name when we finished I left her in the bedroom and went to find _____ but she wasn't there, she was nowhere to be found.

Ignorance isn't always bliss you can't always believe what you hear and sometime you can't even believe what you see, always trust the gut instincts butterflies never lie.

⋄ (Anything is possible in the inner circle, the best of everything, all the money you can make, the prettiest women, most expensive cars, the biggest house on the block anything is possible inside the inner circle, and almost everything is free, free this, V.I.P. that, women falling all over themselves just to belong to someone who's a part of the inner circle, high society types with all the underground connections you could ever dream of, ALMOST no one said no to the people who belong to the inner circle, it was almost like saying no to the inner circle was like breaking the law, it almost never happen, almost. (I need more examples of high society living) The best drugs imaginable and it was always free the best champagne, the best cigars, the finest cloths, and it was like everyone was high all the time, their drug of choice some liked uppers, while others liked downers, some drink, some smoke perscription drugs everywhere, drug cocktails all around and it was always enough drugs to go around, and it was already paid for, the inner circle paid for everything, they cut the price from the merchandise to supply the parties that seemed to go on for days, in a very good if you know what I mean, it was like if you left or went to sleep you would miss the best part of the party, and only hear about the details later. This was nothing like what I saw early before I was excepted into the inner circle, there were no fights except for friendly bullshit, and the regular friend arguments, the inner circle seemed, like the inner circle, at that time for me was perfection, more then perfection it seemed more and more like a dream then reality, it was something I wanted to get use to, living a the best of life were there were no worried, the game they owned the shit it was like there was nothing they couldn't do, anything was possible, anything.) (Living the highlife)

⋄ Anyone worthy to be in the inner circle was apart of the inner circle, and the inner circle, and the inner circle didn't just consist of street hustlers, killers, and drug dealers, no no no this was high scale, high society. I mean docters not answering their phone calls to wasted to save anyone's life, lawyers having the time of their lives handing out business cards talking to people about their cases and traffic tickets, real estate executives, quoting prices on the hottest real estate around financial consultants giving out savings plans for a bigger brighter future I mean everything was inside the inner circle you'd be the dumbest person alive to say no to someone inside the inner circle together the had so much money that they could literally pay almost anyone to say yes to almost anything. Business likes for business types, it was all inside the inner circle, and mingaling a one of the inner circles parties was a most especaily if you wanted to gain pull power and knowledge. You could feel the pulse of energy and power from the people inside the party, it was like my anicheration never happen, and I was now part of the family of friends who all belonged inside the inner circle. Living the high life at one of the inner circle parties, you'd never know what you'd find on the other side of the door exotic women in little eitty bitty bikinis searching fun and a good time, underground business meetings, women and men powdering their noses, men running around drunk looking for their dates so they could get a little piece of action, gambling winner takes all you know the rules, here we play for keeps. I was introduced to everyone who was there everyone from the super models to the chief of police who did all but said nothing, just another part of the inner circle, the inner circle ran everything and it seemed that nothing would work without the connection found within the inner circle. You couldn't pay to have a better time it was like I stepped into a room filled to the brim with lottery winners still in shock not knowing what to do with their winnings.

- Stick with me and you'll say fuck a piece of the pie, I want it all
- When do I start
- You already have,

Main character and his student go through the anishiation process and take care of business according to plan, they just got finished taking care of a few guys who stole from them and lied about it (I'm just breaking in the new face) after handling business, acting like nothing happened and no one got shot they jump back into the car and drive off.

- I never done that before, that's the first time I've ever seen any one get killed before, what did they do.

- They stole from me, and stealing from me is the same as stealing from you in this line of work, and once they get away with it the first time and the second time, and then maybe even third time, I'm the one that has to go collect, it's a dirty job but somebody has to do it

- They come and they go (handing a bag to the new face (need names for characters))

Don't get none of that on the floor I just got the car cleaned they other day.

- They were theives and now they're dead, they weren't in the inner circle, you don't have nothing to worry about, they broke the rules and they had to pay, you play you pay that's how it goes, you have to play by the rules around

- here we own the streets around here

- How do I know I'm not outside the circle, and you would put a bullet

- I let you in the car didn't I, trust me I pick you your alright with me, I've heard nothing but good things about you, trust me you have nothing to worry about, I'm here to teach you the ropes and help you become part of our empire. Those men had it coming they went against us they've been stealing for years now, and it had to come to a stop sooner or later. They knew they had it coming. See in this game if you break the rules, there's always somebody to make you pay, money talks and they didn't let the money talk to me. They didn't think we knew who it was stealing, but around here we know everything and we alwayz take care of business, business is what we do. You can't let people nickle and dime you out of house and none if you do, you won't have anything left. That's why you have to cut the head off the snake before it bits you instead of after you've been biten, you'll live longer that way.

- Welcome to the inner circle where everythings possible and anything, I mean anything can happen and most of it usually does.

◆ Before we go in forget what you saw in the (store house, or building) they were outside the family, you have nothing to worry about, it never happened

◆ (He could never forget the sounds of bullets and screams echoing inside that little room and the flashes of lights and the smell of gun powder, lives lost over change, nothing he could do could changed what happen inside that room, thankful now he was a part of the inner circle) (This is where the characters met the new addition to the group. The new member has past his test and made it back alive)

Notes

‣ Scareface

Started with nothing, immagrint from another county where his life was constantly in danger coming into this new world of America where anything is possible, where his rights would be appreciated, and his life would be valued and accepted no matter the cost, no matter what happened to him in America his life wouldn't be in jeopary. While trying to make mince meat in America the Land of the Free, working as a dishwasher from Cuba, with an old friend from Cuba, his friend who came with him to America from Cuba to escape presurcution, they met a known drug dealer who show him "Tony Montana" how good American life can be when you know the right people. Scareface "Tony Montana" and his friend who came with him to America got offered a job running drugs for me, giving him and his friend a chance to come up in the world, TO MAKE SO REALLY MONEY. So he quit his job, him and his friend and went to work for him. On his first job Scareface and three other friends of his went to make an exchange the money for the product and either the man that hired them or the people they met inside the apartment turned against them, trying to take the money and the dope, and their lives, they chopped up one person in the shower while handcuffed, and next was Scareface when his friend who came with him from Cuba came in and saved his life, and when Scareface got free from his handcuff he followed the last surviver out into the street and face to face, put one bullet into his head, and then gave the money and the dope to the boss of the person who hired them, showing him respects and gaining respect for him and his crew at the same time, respect first, money later. Scareface figured out that the person who hired him and his crew, set them up to die, and the tables turned whom Scareface and his crew came back alive instead of in body bags. Scareface meet his new bosses girlfriend that night a dope mans true prize is his loyal bitch, his prize pasation Scareface had to have her at any cost she was a pretty shoby, stuck up, greedy bitch, who loved coke, I guess she remined him of himself in a way opposites attract, she stood for or having her meant having money, power and respect not everyone could afford or handle a woman like her, her lifestyle would kill some people who couldn't find a way to handle or control him but I remembered she loves coke, money, and she's strongly attracted to power, all she did was please her man in the bedroom and spend money, she never made money that way her man's job.

‣ After meeting the man in charge the man who pays the man who pays them money started to roll in, the more money he and his crew made for the bossman the more respect and money they made, nothings for free

‣ playing Russian rulet like he said "never underestimate the other man's greed (When death knocking at the door. I hope you don't answer it)

‣ Somebody once told me never to borrow money you can't afford to pay back.

‣ Never burn a bridge you may need to cross later.

• <u>Never bite the hand that feeds you: Actions speak louder then words.</u>

• <u>Keep business, business even when it's personal: Don't expect a man to respect you if you don't show that man respect: Never ask someone to do something for you, you aren't willing to do whatever you asked to be done.</u>

• <u>Don't be so quick to judge others you never know what you might learn.</u>

Notes   Scareface note

<u>Keep your money at the streets</u> for movie

Scareface and his crew become to big for the bossman, him and his crew started to take over some of his clientel putting a dent in the bossmans pocket and putting moves on his girl, so the bossman ordered a hit on Scareface. After Scareface met the bossmans boss the producer of the product, and after avading the atempt on his life Scareface rounded up his crew and confronted the bossman inside his office with off duty police officers present. And after a few brief words <u>Scareface killed the bossman for putting the hit out on him and the off duty police officer for helping</u> plan the hit. After that Scareface took over the Bossman's business and <u>got premission to conduct business</u> as usually as long as Scareface didn't fuck him business would run smooth <u>by this time the money is rolling</u> in for Scareface and his crew, Scareface is now with the women who was with the boss before Scareface, <u>the women he could now afford</u> and then Scareface gets arrested for laundering money and has to do a favor for a friend before he goes to jail for the Big Boss the one who's incharge of it all a real smooth cat a person who likes nice things and would kill you with a smile on his face a person with class great edacite a true business straight through the heart, he was trying to teach Scareface how to run the business in the states to keep the business running smooth, but the Big Boss man told Scareface not to fuck him and the favor for a favor thing never happened, Scareface was suppose to kill someone or drive while the Big Bossman tired hand kill someone and because of the person who was suppose to die had his kids with him, Scareface killed the person who was suppose to kill the person who was suppose to die (killed the hired hand, the hitman) so the Big Bossman sent his crew to handle the situation and they showed Tony Montanta <u>go out in a blaze of gun shots grenades and glory</u>

• <u>Never make a promise you can't keep</u>

• Alwayz expect the unexpected

• <u>If you stay loyal you'll go a long way in this line of business, if you run in to any problems at all you know who to talk to.)</u> If you live hard you have to prepare to die hard that just how it is, not everyone has the heart to take the chances we make or face the problems we face, this life is as tuff as nails and cold as ice we have to make the most of what we have, and it's never easy making something out of nothing. Life is hard and then it gets harder, with only a few breaks in between to catch our breaths that's why we have to make every second count, if we don't somebody else will, and I can't afford to take that lose I got too much to lose to let the next man get over on me. That's why we own the street. We keep the family happy and everyone keeps their ears to the street

We're only as strong as our weakest link, and we can't afford to break too much competition out here, too many people who want to see us, too many people trying to take our place in line. We can't afford to show in this line of work there's no time for weakness, only the strong survive out here in these bloody streets. Time is money and we never know how much we have left, that why we can't afford to show mercy. There's no time for remorse, in this life there is no second chances if we don't act or react the next man will. Do you want to wait for them to make a move and leave your brains splattered on the streets, with your family and everything you love ripped to pieces? Can you stand and watch everything you built fall right on top of you? I know I can't, I refuse to loose, out here it's survival at all cost, living in this doggy dog world, you have to become the top dog, and you can't play with the big dogs if you pee like a puppy. We have to control the block, we have to control the city. I want the whole state in my back pocket, and if I didn't have help I'd be out here getting it myself. Time doesn't wait for long. I know time won't want for me, my heads on the line everyday I don't get breaks in the world I live in there's no time for sleep. When you run with the animals you have to learn how to become one or die trying. Out here it's survival at all cost, life or death, kill or be killed, and I can't afford to loose I got to much to loose and everything to gain, you see that corner store, I bought that those apartment complexes down town and on the west side I bought. I even bought the grocrey stores down the block. I want it all and I can't take by myself, I need people I can trust, people who give their life for me knowing I would do the same people who won't turn against me like a mad dog, no matter what the cost maybe. Most of the people around here don't even know what loyalty is, some of them don't even respect their own mamma's, but I'd be damed if they don't respect me

• If you stay loyal, and stick to the game plan, you will earn your own piece of the pie, and you can eat it any way you want, all you have to do is stick to the game plan and we can own all this, as far as the eye can see, if they don't want their money then they should bring their money to me.

• You'd be amazed what gets some people through the day, for me it's the feel and the smell of money and a beautiful women, but if you ask me I'd take a million dollers over a pretty face any day. Some people it's their children that gets them through the day, or that comfortable chair with the ass grooves and a fat joint, or that drink at the bar after work, and for some it's that snow, I'm telling no matter what season these people love to see it show. Money don't lie, no matter what you sell if it's good, and people know about, and able to buy, then they'll eat it up like a hot plate on Sunday. The point in this game is to beat the competition no matter if it's the quality or price. If you want to make money you have to make money it's as simple as that money don't grow on trees around here. They get one taste of this shit and they want to buy from anyone else, the cleanest, purest out there and we own the market, so we own the price we can either drop the price or raise it as high as we want and since we control the market we own the game. They can't help but fuck with us.

to the belly of the beast, it's hell out here, <u>you have to plan every move carefully, to avoid getting burned</u>. What we do out here stays out here, the less people know about our livies outside of our family the better out here <u>what we know can</u> hurt and even <u>kill</u>. It's first come first serve, we have to make sure we don't run out, there to much competition, we have to control the market at all cost.

◆ When the shit hits the fan, most people can't handel the smell

◆ When plans don't go as planed most of these motherfuckers out here wouldn't think twice about leaving you in the dust. It's sad but true most of the people we know only care about self, it's all about money out here and they can't afford to think about anything else, that's why we have no choice but to stick to our guns with a itchy finger to protect our heads, life is short and we only get one roll of the dice.

◆ We have no choice we have to strike while the iron's hot there's no room for error in these streets, one wrong move can cost you your life or worse we can't afford to show mercy <u>I bet my head on a silver platter, if it comes down to you are them, they'll go for self every time, in this game that's how the cookie crumbles, it's a short life and it's easy to loose, but how good it feels to win. To me it's just another day, another doller in the belly of the beast</u> a lot of people loose it all out here, only a few really make it I mean really make it, most of the time this fast cash doesn't last long enough to spend most of the time, has to be more the one hustle there has to be more then one road, one avenue to success, that's why I keep my hands in, everything I see, like a little kid with his hand in the cookie jar, or in grandmas birthday cake. You hear me I want it all, and I'm don't mine sharing, but hear what I say only with a chozen few, most the people on the outside of the circle can't be trusted, and trust is hard to find, but let the truth be told I'm always on the hunt for loyal, trustworthy people, but I've seen alot of people loose their life to the game, man I tell you it's a cold world out here so either turn up the heat or go home because I hate to tell you most people don't survive out here without a level head strong backbone and a great heart, that's how it's gotta be respect, honesty and loyalty, without that those three rules, we're nothing but a sac of shit waiting to get flushed down the toilet. Money rules down here, out here freezing in hell, tell them if they can't stand the heat then stay the fuck out of these streets.

◆ I ain't the devil but I know how to act like one, you gotta guard your pocket watch your back and hold your heart close no matter what it is these streets are heartless they know no remorse and the give no money. Money rules the streets can't do without it, making the root of all evil in the belly of the beast is an every day thing, there's no room for mercy out here, no room at all.

◆ I notice your knack to make money, I like they way you handel yourself, but more importantly I like the way you handle business. You and me are a lot a like if you haven't already noticed. I'm here to show you how to make <u>real money</u>, the kind of money you only hear about in movies, the kind of money we all dream about, if you want I can help you make all your dreams come true, faster then you think.

INNER CIRCLE MOVIE STUFF

Find a better name if possible   www.IMEEM.com

Movie notes
(Details matter the most tell the story)

Movies to research:
New Jack City
Sugar Hill
Hoodlum
In too Deep
(take notes pro's & con's)
password
swordfish
punisher
read book (Even Steven)
Blow
Hardball
Street Kings
City of God
48 Hrs (chase scene)
Carlito's Way
1 and part 2
Pulp Fiction
Training Day

Bronx tail
Lost Boys
Hear death knocking
But you can't come in

Narrated (some parts)

Objects to and/or put fear in the hearts of viewers and to teach the rules and regulation to the Dope Game it's a cold world out here in these streets money, power, respect "I want respect first "money later"

• <u>Write a story</u> to compare or just come close to the <u>classics</u>: <u>Scareface</u>, <u>Godfather's</u>, <u>Goodfellas</u>, <u>Belly</u>, <u>Usually Suspects</u> <u>Seven</u>, <u>Beans</u>, <u>Shottas</u>. Stay as true to life as possible to delivery the life in the dope game how hard it is, how to live the life, what strain and stress the ganstas hold. How quick life is for some, how the game traps those who don't want anything better than living the life of a ganster, and those who can't seem to climb out, most important <u>Monopalizing the Dope Game</u>: "cut throat kill or be killed If you ain't with me then your against me," "I can't wait for you to make your move" "I'll work first fuck later them niggas might kill me" <u>Main character</u> must be ruthless holds no mercy <u>within</u> the dope game I got to much on the line to wait for them to make their move this shit is like a game of chess, sometime you have to sacrifice a playa to win. "I'm the motherfuckin king out here these niggas can't touch me etc

• Circle of tight friends one or two must stay faithful at all cost no matter what. "I never forget a good deed" "No friends. No foes just money" I'll double up now and buy yo ass later." Nigga I gotta eat ain't no time to sleep when yo own the streets these nigga stand in line waiting to take my place that why I don't give a fuck fuck em all and the hollow tips fall. I kill them before they even think about killing me I got what they dream about

"I respect myself and good business I can't afford bad blood problems are bad for business"

*Flashbacks to educate movie watchers about the characters history their background what really makes them who the are and why they act the way they do! Bring realness into the characters to help depth and realness (what time frame)

⁺ niggas die for less, niggas kill over pennies I don't have time to wait until they get the upper hand, this competition is cold blooded that's why I'm a cold blooded motherfucka dare these niggas to come test my nuts.

⁺ Someone crossed the line and broke the rules and regulations goes to jail and get murdered by his cellmate "check mate nigga" he broke a very important rule

⁺ For some it's very hard to keep a lid on their anger "human nature" that killer instinct you know sometimes the inner beast gets control of the situation and you never knew what a person will do when their anger gets the best of them. I try not to let my anger get the best of me but no one's perfect.

⁺ Inorder for us to remain successful we must have order even in the mist of cahos don't let these problems cloud your judgement stick to the plan and everthing will fall in place. Once you let go and let the cahos consume you we all lose, you have to stay focused don't let them get the best of you or we all fail and I can't afford to loose. In order for us to beat the competition we all have to stick to the plan until there is no competition. We have to outlast them all, if they stay out there for 24 hours we have to be out there 24/7 if they cut it down and lower the price, we supply the uncut, if the own the street then we buy Da Block. We have to own the market then we control the price, now tell me how can we loose when they have no choice but to buy from us.

⁺ I can't seem to climb out of hell, it feels like I've been swimming in quicksand my whole life the more I try to climb out the deeper I seem to sink shit I'm trying my best not to drown take a walk in my shoes and you'll find out how hard life can get, you think this shit is easy, you think you can handle all this, you think you can carry the load that these streets put on my back you wouldn't last a day in my shoes, if you're ready to handle the load, if you're really ready to sit in my chair then show me, talk is cheap and we can't afford to loose. I've been the man on top for too many years seen some many fall and never climb out of the pit, they come and they go and I'm still here watching the new comers to the game, these new beeties to the game who think their all that, most of them would shoot their own mothers in the back if it meant they would see an extra doller. The game changes and you have to learn to change with it, some can but most don't make it shit even these old heads around here sometimes forget that even they can be taken out at anytime, there no time for laziness in the life we live, there no room for mistakes, one wrong move can cause a city to fall, do you want to be responsible for that, can you be the one to send your bother into the pit praying that he can find his way out. I've been there and done that, and it's never easy, your not ready to carry the load there's too much at stake we have too much to lose, do you know how many people would kill to take over, they propable all would. I can't give them the chance there's no time to sleep at the top.

*

I'm sick of these motherfuckers out here talking shit all yall pussy bitch made niggas can suck my dick, just let me know how you want it nigga I could put that ass in a bag or box clips already ready already get ready to catch shots, but if you ask me nigga you'd look better in a box

Staying hardcore prepared and ready for war ready to even the score if you play hardcore then you die hardcore I hear you out there talking all that shit all yall hating niggas can suck my dick and you know I stay sick with it so if you want it pussy nigga I got no problem I'm already to deliver so please come get some I aim for the head nigga ready for redrum. There's a million in one ways to say fuck you got yo body in the crossheirs ready to bust through never thought I meet a pussy nigga soft as you, you don't have to ask me I already got a box for you get ready to catch shots pussy nigga out here fucking with these niggas harder then crack rocks got the crossheirs aimmed and locked watch that head nigga you bout to get knock fuck the chest plate I aim for the head to make your face turn blue and your body leak red I don't give a fuck about you pussy nigga to me you better off dead you can keep your money nigga I aim for the head before I throw lead and I stay hard nigga the type to fill you up and piss on your head I don't give a fuck about you I can do without ya got you in the crossheir nigga and I'm glad I found ya

Rewrite   *   *   *   *   *

Had me fuck up on <u>Howdall</u> bouncing off the wall, they made my cell feel like hell. I'm sane and they can tell held waiting for my court date with no bail what is it about me you despies, keeping a lid on me praying for my demise now I'm outnumbered I wonder why they long to die and catch the kiss of death and the long kiss goodbye and out gun hard life got me on the run chasing the raising sun it's either hell or jail go hard or go home now I got a bandana around my mouth ready to stand to deliver chrome tight more explosive then dynomite. I'm sorry sir these bitch nigga most likely won't survive the night I'm underground type of nigga caught by stage fright, but fuck that I need to spit my life, and nothing excites me more then hitting these niggas up hard core, putting slugs through meaning making these nigga uglyer then before I'm sleeping with fourty four always prepared for war leave these niggas sleeping six feet under the floor I send it before what is it about me you despies they pray and pray for my downfall praying for my demies I know these hate me busting before I can see the white in their eyes yo death ain't no surprise to me, these niggas still alive surprisingly face to face with my number ace to earse yo???

It really don't matter I can push yo head back homie split yo brain and watch your brain matter split and splatter my back's against the wall homie so yo life don't matter I ain't shit to loose life or death bitch nigga you choose, make that ass snooze and lose my bones might break but my bullets don't loose you can pick the ammo of choice I'll leave the size of the caliber up to you when the beast is out of the cage it ain't nothing I can do name the time and the place I'll leave death all up to you you tried to fuck me so I'll let the bullets fuck you it's your fate homie your life is up to you my back against the wall so you know I don't give a fuck about you the line drawn, it's your choice so my nigga do what you do it's your life homie but I'm waiting on you

*

Falling through space and time feeling the weight of the world and the pressure of everyday life bring me down, and I can't see the ground there's no end in sight, no end to the frustration only dark no light, fatigued by the pressure that life brings, hunted by father time and the seconds that follow falling through space and time trying to hold on to the time line of life wondering how did time pass me by, where did I stop living, and where did I begin to watch my life drift away, with no gleamer of light in sight and nothing real to hold on too only space and time and the weight of the world that haunts me. Seconds turn into minutes and minutes turn in to hours and hours become centuries. I have forgotten how long I've been falling the only thing left remaining with me is past memories of a time left behind, memories that give me the chance to face the face of mine, with no light in sight I don't even know which way is down, falling through space, through time watching the sounds of death move around up or down, doesn't matter to me falling in love all over again with my precious memories of a time that once was, searching for a familiar face and a familiar place to visit and roam thoughts that take me away, and for a second I feel like I'm home. Falling through space and time wondering where did the time go, searching to find the life of mine falling through time and space holding on to my timeline. I'm I gone and forgotten lost in space trapped by time just falling away from life or am I trapped in the minds of others who can't forget a light like mine. So alone in the drift downward with no life in sight. I've been falling for so long I forget how life is like without my light. There's so much darkness that surrounds me here falling through space and time, hearing the echos of the voice of mine more than just a dream, and yet less then reality searching through my memories, falling through space with time and me, trying to catch a brief vision of life's landscape or a moment not yet forgotten a picture to picture or something loved that has been lost through time but never forgotten, a loved one something to hold on to as I continue to fall with the weight of the world ontop on me as I continue to fall through space and time with a light I can't see, trying my best to hold on to the timeline of a life that once was mine searching for happiness, a friendly handshake or a loving hug or a entimate moment spent with someone close to the heart, a life gone but no forgotten, I don't know where to start. Falling through space and time holding on to the timeline continously missing the life of mine counting the seconds watching the minutes pass searching for something to hold on to as I continue to search through my past that passed on with the weight of the world on my shoulders and life behind me if I ever slip away from your mind you know exactly where to find me holding on to the timeline searching through this life of mine

11-29-08 before

I'm there to help you, catch you when you fall, I'll be there to hold you up when you need to stand tall, I'm the one that's always here everytime you call, I'm the one who's been with you, and watched you go through it all. Older then the sands of time, stronger then the light of the sun if your wishes are at all possible then they shall be done, you can find me everywhere and a piece of me in everyone here to help you in your time of need until the job is done here to cool you off even in the hottest summer sun, here to warm you in the coldest of winter nights, there to guide you home when your heart sings to me, watching you go through it all, here to help you stand up before you start to fall, I'm here even though sometimes you can't tell, I'm always here when your sleeping watching you inhale. I'm not always here when you wake up but I'll alway leave a piece of myself with you, you don't think I hear what you say, but I here to let you know I do. I'll be here to hold you up in your time of need, watching things grow watering a tree remembering the seed, strong and firmly in place, I'm here to comfort you while time takes its place everything that starts always has to end, but remember I'm always here to listen, until the end, your friend

**

What you staring at playa potna ain't no pussy over here why you looking at me funny ain't no pussy over here ain't no pussy over here ain't no pussy over here yo face wide open ain't no pussy over here ain't no pussy you got me fucked up playa potna ain't no pussy over here ain't no pussy over here.

* *

Ain't no pussy over here playa potna it's best you let it drip dry ain't no faking ain't no fronting and it ain't no punking me sorry playa potna I have no hoe card to let go out we can piece up fist to cuffs and let the dogs go throw I do this shit for real playa potna we can let the funk show if you want to antie up on anna then bitch let it go get in where you fit in I got pounds to blow with a big booty cutie with miles to go so why you looking at me funny if you ain't ready tooo if you really want it potna I can give you what you asked for and much more ain't no pussy over here just coke cola models that pop bottels with blunts to share I'm right here playa potna I ain't going nowhere you can serve the beef if you want to I'm ready to eat it up then get back to my bottel after I beat it up so if you really want it potna get ready to antie up sitting over here with toy dogs ready to eat up I'm ready when you ready let me know when it's time to antie up ain't no pussy over here just hustlas killers and dope dealers over here with no time for bitch made shit I think you left your balls at home I'll give you time to go and get ain't no pussy over here I ain't going nowhere playa potna I'm standing right here. Yo face wide open we can handle it right lay you down where you stand for fucking with this man right here leave you swimming where you stand no time to play around round here niggas get socked and get their heads on floor around here sorry playa potna ain't no pussy round here why you looking at me funny niggas get stompped around here I'd hate to put you in ICU but if you keep talking shit it will be hell to pay when I see you ain't no pussy over here playa potna so let it drip dry my nigga you know how I do ain't no pussy over here playa potna you can do what you feel I'm cool high as fuck I don't give a shit about you it's best you get in where you fit it before me and my nigga stomp you I'm high as motherfucker it's too many bitches around for me to think about you I'd advise you to pick one up before somebody lays that ass down I'm a grown ass man high as fuck with no time to play around so knucke up shut the fuck up I'm tried of fucking around niggas thick in the club playa potna be careful before you drown. I ain't no pussy over here

*rewrite

Keep it poppin playa potna we keep it pimping over here no time to play around time is money around here watch you head and prepare to bread if you get caught slippin around here some niggas don't give a fuck because you ain't from around here we keep it popin playa potna that's how we pimp over here so it pimping around here what's poppin playa potna we keep it pimping over here pop colours and clock dollers ain't nothing but hos bitches and baller out here so if you ain't about making money homeboy it's best you stay yo ass from around here living in a place where bitches and ho's come a dime a dozen and ballers kick back and watch them big booties shake we put it down around here kicking plants around making the world shake we some heavy home run hitters hustlas and dome spitters you ain't know homeboy I'm the pick of the litter eating these haters up like a home cooked soul food dinner if you fake homeboy then my realm you better not enter not disrespect homeboy I want more then sardines from dinner coming from a place where we smoke trees all day kickback and move that winter where only the ballers can ball and bring home dinner out here in these street we have no choice but to keep it professional nigga it's hard around here and we choose to be criminal sorry homeboy we stay croked around here I ain't been straight for a while time is money so if you ain't got it for me then don't even press redail I ain't new at this homeboy I been stuck in this game for a while but if everything on the up and up then you know what number to dial my money don't sleep and neither does my handy four five I always keep it handy just incase they try to creap everybody knows when your making that money move it ain't no time to sleep we open twenty four seven keeping up the phone before the voice mail gets a chance to beep catch me riding around town with my business and something loaded up and ready up under the seat I'm sorry homeboy I got a price you can't beat I gotta feed the belly when it's time to eat.

time to reup we sell out twice a week

You can feel the flames and the heat from under the feet protecting what matters when brain matter matters the most from the streets to the highway until it's time to let shit coast from coast to coast from state to state city after city keeping my nina with me hoping nobody crosses the line before I hit the state line and get mine living the life of dope dealing killing and penatantary time you can keep yours I'm out here to get mine living the life of crime with the sun to my back I know money loves me every time I come back drop off pick up loving the smell of money I'm a moneymaker loving the feel of the dough you ain't got to ask me for shit I already got what you asked for just hand me the dough and we straight let the money talk and bullshit walk and just feel up the plate loving the feel of crisp stack of hundred doller bills with the heads pointed in the right direction with my iron gripped tight just incase they start flex no hoping them boys don't come and test my nuts out here in these streets driving straight but always feeling like a nut out here with the heat under the seat I'm hot so don't touch me ready to hit the street and sit back and watch the pounds rush me protecting what matters the most when brain matter matters the most turn the music up roll the windows up and just coast back to the state they call insanity I'm too hot to hold these niggas can't handle me with my money on my mind at all time listening to the music loving to press rewind I'd rather make money then waste time I stay focused on the grind out here to get mine eyes on the clock I hate wasting my time big time now no time to nickle and dime trying to live a life with less grimm and more shine putting myself in the way of hard time I hate suggling so I'm stuck living in the world of crime I stay hot looking for a way to cool off before I overheat and explode. I'm too hot to handle to hot to hold I hope I never see the day when making more gets old it's best to hold money in stack until my pockets explode I got a hold on the grind and I can't let go sticking to the streets watching my pockets grow I got to play it smart and make my fast cash last hoping these haters from around the block don't catching my ass life is too short so I'm staying on the grind stacking up my chips with no time to waste time I'm too hot to handle to hot to hold trying to cool off before my glock explodes living in a world where time is money protecting mine in this life of crime ain't nothing about my life funny on the the grind with no time to waste stuck in the life and addicted to the taste of fast cash watching the hours past waiting on the next shipment I gotta pay the rent it's too late now too much money spent making moves from state to state doing what I gotta do to fill my plate playing the game and I can't afford to lose loving the smell of money and I hate to lose stuck in the fast lane and I got the pedal to the floor living the hard life if you want so more because I'm too hot to handle too hot to hold trying to cool off before the police take control I love making money so everything else's on hold I don't know about you but to me making money never gets old stuck in the fast lane and I can't compliane stuck to the grind living a life that's insane. Out here doing what I do to make shit shaka rattle and roll stuck in the grind everything else on hold with a grip on life making sure shit don't get out of control playing the game smart before I end up frozen living the life I'v chosen making that money move too deep in the game now and no time to lose feeling the heat from under the seat hitting the streets with a price you can't beat because I'm too hot to hold and too much to handle eyes open glock cocked with a price you can't beat. I stay hot you can see the flames- from under the seat

mind, body, soul
imagination, vessel, spirit

2 half to a whole
the good
the bad
always different (without the other the other would rise to exist (total))

(2) TRENCHES

Everybody gave up on me except for me, even though I'm stuck in the trenches, I know the bottoms not for me, I can't give up on life even if life gives up on me.] I keep my head to the <u>sky</u> holding onto life watching my life fly <u>bye</u>, just a street soldier searching for a piece of the <u>pie</u>, ready to give life just one more <u>try</u> trying to touch greatness one more time before I die, just a street soldier stuck in the trenches until it's my time to <u>die</u>, watching out for death trying to give life one more <u>try</u> just another street soldier stuck to the grind holding on to life until the I <u>die</u> stuck in the trenches watching my life <u>fly bye</u>

The good the bad and the ugly

These motherfuckers faker then a three doller bill, hating for thrills, my heart so cold now I give myself chills, never fake always real they love to hate so what's the deal; beef I'll eat up every last meal 100% until I'm finish with every last deal always real I never hate for thrills my best friend is the steal and stacked crisp hundred doller bills

*Mr. Deadman walking don't you hear this psycho talkin I hope you get a chance to tell me how it taste to catch a malit off cocktail straight to the face, while I watch you run around like a chicken with its head cut off burning up the place, I hope you love the smell of the place, watching your flesh burn and sizzle and fall off burning to bright and no one can turn the lights off, send you to your maker after I cermate ya, and burn yo house down, no evidence needed you know how I get down no messing around spread your ashes around after the flames put you out, ain't no surprise he was burnt alive but not buried I could care less about you resting in peace is secondary, can't hear you talking now Mr. burn to a crisp I don't see you walking now you just a piece of charcoal now, I knew you die sooner or later I hope you savored the flavor before it was time to go, watching you scream in aganie trying to climb out the window, watching you try to put your self out in the sink, watching you in a blaze of glory is all you can do for me looks like your too hot for me. If you wanted something else to drink you should have asked me, just let the motherfucka burn life had it chance now it's deaths turn, I told you to leave me alone, now your too hot to handle and your burning all alone, you should be more when your dying in your own. just sit here and watch the fire until your all gone

I do things you can't see

I'm used to getting locked over you see, just another day another doller another day in the life to me, selling Kane and Mary Jane doing things you can't see, if you see a familar face in the crowd it's usually me, I been here so long they forgot about me, but how could you forget about me, when you got caught up and was scared to call momma to bail you out you picked up and call me. You see I do things you can't see, just going through life until life goes through me. If you remember correctly you got yo connect through me, I think that's how you forgot about me, money changed things, that's why I do things you can't see, you might be the type of nigga to bitch out and snitch on me, you see I think that's why you don't want to make money with me, you see I think big and you still nickle and diming you see, trying to take the bitch that rightfully chose me, see that's why I do things you can't see, the same nigga to smile in my face will be the same nigga to turn around and snitch on me, all because I do things you can't see, hating what you see when you look over me scared to bring yo bottom bitch around because she might choose me, see that's why I do things you can't see because if you could see what I see nigga you might just hate on me, just remember I didn't choose the bitch, the bitch chose me. I think that's why the nigga forgot about me all because of the things he can't see, you see selling Kane and Mary Jane ain't nothing new to me, when started to bad up the team potna you should have told me, I guess it's because of the things I can't see, but I don't hate the game so why would you hate me, but getting hated on ain't nothing new to me, it's just another day, another doller, another hustla to me that's why I do things you can't see, because I love money and money loves me, see I just trying to be all that I can be without these niggas out here always trying to hate on me if your bitch ain't with you then she's probably with me that why I do things you can't see, because if you knew your lady loved me you might try to hate on me, if you was from the town we would have stuck together so you could through me, but I see a nigga doing good, trying to put a lid on me, if you were as smart as you thought you was you would've made yo money with me but instead of sticking together like birds of a feather you stepped on toes and turned around a hated on me, see that's why I do things you can't see next time you turn around the nigga on top might just be me, see that's why I do things you can't be, because your the type of nigga that loves to hate on me, selling Kane and Mary Jane is an everyday thang to me, just another day, another doller, just another day in the life for me

* rewrite

Them niggas bleed just like us load up and cockback safety off ready to push they head back ready to get it on nigga don't get yo head cracked

Them niggas make chesse just like us hit em in the pockets, they dope game stop it keep the nine close in case you got pop it

Them niggas Gs just like us, they get handcuffed and arrested put on they knees just like us, they stay strapped up ready to bust in these streets with no trust

Them niggas bleed just like us no love in the dope game pushing niggas out the box that how we slang Kane. Find out how long them niggas can survive without how long they can maintain without the product they slang, holla at how they holla at this is ours they can't slang. Them niggas make cheese just like us no love in the dope game no love in these streets find but how much they hold and where they keep the heat whatever the price is I got it beat find out where they stay I wanta know where them nigga's sleep what city what street. Them niggas Gs just like us, so them niggas ain't scared to bust, find out who they trust in this world with no trust who they slang with who they hang with who they bang with who they smoke blunts to they brain with, ain't no room for them niggas out here we own the street them niggas causing problems slanging Kane bringing the heat let them nigga any price I can beat them niggas sleep just like us catch them nigga slipping waking up with their pockets missing. Take everything you see even the pot in the kitchen hit em where it hurts my pockets dying of thirst I been out here to long putting in work stay loaded up and ready in case you gotta put em in the dirt

They slang hang out here it's time to pull up their skirts. Find out how long they been putting in work

If them niggas can maintain slanging Kane they gotta push my work, make it hard for these niggas make their pockets hurt.

Find out who they sleep with and what they sleep with I know she ain't faithful get close to his bitch make her willing and able when she's willing and able we can't afford the competition. We gotta bring these nigga's in our take these niggas out of the game no matter what our pockets gotta maintain what's had for us is bad for the street which is bad for business out here it's cut throat they fucking with these niggas that don't play these niggas who slang Kane and cut throats ain't no love in these streets we gotta kill their pockets to kill the competition

They have to get in where they fit in they gotta pay to play if they gotta grind they gotta grind our way ain't no love in these streets they gotta pay the price for living the hard life they gotta play with us if they want roll the dice we need a piece if they want a piece of the pie they gotta pay to play my nigga that no lie ain't shit for free I want in no lie these niggas gotta get in where they fit in they gotta pay to play if they want to eat in these streets they gotta grind our way living in these street where niggas die for ya if they want to eat out here they gotta play our way they gotta get in where they fit in and grind the hard way if they want to slang Kane they gotta pay to play, playing in these streets where niggas die everyday

No love like pac fuck em all and let the hollow tips fall why would I give a fuck when it's me against all yall fuck em all and let the hollow tips fall ain't no love when its me against yall fuck em all

Ain't no love just backstabbers snitches and mean mugs killers and dope dealers who go slug for slug. I can't trust no body except for me myself and I everybody stepping over me for a piece of the pie. If you listen to what I say then you know I tell you no lies the truth hurts especially when it's staring you in the face don't turn your back potna keep your eyes open and savor the taste the truth hurts espeacially when it's right in your face. Ain't no love out here just killers and dope dealers trying to make it out the slims out here born and raised on the block and learned to show no fear showing love by turning over battle after battle for those they lost out here living in a world where you can't afford to show fear. Ain't no love eseacially when you live around here. Don't you see we all try to climb out of the pit some spend so much time climbing and forget they keep a lid on the pit getting so little for so much time spent. Some let go others raise to the top why let go when your so close to the top, holding back pain they can't afford to show trying to hold on before they have to let go, ain't no love in these streets people die everyday over gunplay looking at the world from a different view when it's you against me. Keeping my head up trying to move on it's hard in these streets sometimes I can barely move trapped in a world where it's hard to carry on, keeping my head up trying my best to hold on living in this cold world I got to stay strong trying my best to survive out before I'm gone. There ain't no love out here just sacs cadallac's and broken bottles of beer surviving in a place where you can't afford to show fear trying to climb out of the pit even when death near it's more to life then a sac and a bottle of beer ain't no love around here just broken hearts broken dreams and death around ain't no love around here especially for me living in this cold world with no love for me

Naw bitch fuck you step back before I bunk you naw bitch fuck you step back before I bunk you

[One step two step staying on the grind getting mine in due time I gots to shine eventually getting mine until then I'm staying focused on the grind, hustling all day making money in all ways I gots to shine.]

So give me mines. One step at a time I'm getting mine eventhough hustling takes time I'm staying on the grind until they break or take mine staying motavated keeping money on my mine I gots to shine, won't let nothing hold me back climbing to the top until the bottom calls me back I gots to shine, making whats mine holding tight to the grind I'm getting mine in due time, taking everyday one step at a time hoping for a life of luxury so I can relax in the sunshine. I gots to shine staying on the grind waiting for the world to to give me mine, out here hustling all day taking the long way making money in all ways living for the day I tommorow I might be gone so I'm staying on the grind until somebody call me home living in a cold world hoping I can survive it on my own hoping I have enough time before somebody calls me home. I gots to shine out here to get mine staying on the grind I'm getting mine in due time, taking every day step by step never knowing how much time I have left. Passed life now I'm waiting for death hoping my life doesn't fly bye when I'm sky high one foot in the my other hand to the sky knowing one day we live and the next day we die. So I'm staying on the grind living life sky high looking at my watch, watching the time fly bye. I gots to shine taking life one day at a time hoping I can relax sitback and enjoy the sunshine I gots to shine eventually getting mine holding to mine before they take or break mine, staying on the grind until I make or break mine I gots to shine out here putting in work trying of struggling when this nine to five don't work. I'm getting mine in due time until then I'm staying focused on the grind I'm getting me I gots to shine so I can kickback relax and enjoy the sunshine so give me mine

I don't just talk about living the hard life I really live this shit. My life ain't sweat staying focused on the grind trying to make ends meet surviving in these mean streets. I wouldn't wish my life on nobody a day in my shoes ain't nothing nice everyday grinding paying the price to live life trying to stay focused trying to climb out of the pullpit my life is hard broken and scared trying to find a way out of the bullshit. Sick and tried of being sick and tried trying to make it to the top with all this stress on me living with this strain on my brain living in this world where I can't be me, why won't they let me be me. Trying to climb out but they keep pulling me back in. How can I win in this world of sin, living a world where I was built to lose holding my balls in my hands with nothing to prove stuck in the grind living this life of mine staying in the grove, taking life one step at a time I'm getting mine searching my piece and my peace of mind hoping to find mine in due time trying to shine in a world that's unkind trying to stay clean but dirt seems to find me trying to shake off the fake that hate me I'm too real living this life sharpen harder then steal stuck in the grove with nothing to prove and everything to lose wondering what life has against me living in this cruel world trying to be me, trying to stay strong with all this bullshit around me. I have have to find a way to win climb out of the pullpit and escape this world of sin. A man is only skin muscle and bone trying to climb to the top so I can finally sit on my throne living in this world surrounded by people but yet I still feel all alone searching for a place to call home staying focused on the grind living in a world all it's own the only thing protecting me myself and I is clip and my chrome taking my life one step at a time staying on the grind waiting for the world to give me mine searching peace and piece of mine surrounded by hate living in a world that ain't mine staying on the grind waiting for the world to give me mine living this hard life and paying the price to roll the dice a day in my life ain't nothing nice alot of heartake and pain stress and strain trying to clean and dry and avoid the rain with all this madness on my brain it's hard for me to hold on. I can't let go bullshit seems to follow me everywhere I go watching the smoke bounce off the window the stress and strain of this hard life feel like it will never let go a day in my life

battered broken and bruised fighting a losing battel and I refuse to lose staying focused on the grind waiting for my time to shine on the grind until the world gives me mine standing on the edge trying to walk away some die can't handle the pressure but to me it's just another day living with killers and dope dealer surrounded bye gun play just another day in the life I live trying to survive in these mean streets staying focused on the grind trying to make ends meet living in a world that wasn't ment from me I know this life of bullshit isn't the life for me trying to climb out of the pullpit and make life right for me I guess staying on the grind all the time is the life for me until things go right it's the grind and the hard life for me how can I stop to smell the roses when bullshit is all I see I guess it's the life of crime for me until I reach the top or until you see the end of me living in a world that wasn't built for me I guess all I got is my balls and my word my chrome and my clip with me I guess living the hard life was just ment for me, what do except from me when all I see is hatred and the bullshit that surounds me living in this world that wasn't built for me hoping the hard life won't be the death of me give me whats mines you can keep whats left of me tried of these motherfucker testing me these hating motherfuckers will be the death of me. A day in my shoes ain't nothing nice living the hard life hoping it don't take my life staying focused on the grind surviving in these cold streets taking life step bye step until ends meet.

I'm allergic to these fake bitches
so bitch get from around me, don't
crowd me fake bitch you can't do
shit for me, no time for you I'm
too busy tring to do me so fake
bitch get from around me so I can
do me stop crowding fake bitch
get from around me

Walking to own death
Gripping my nut sac and
I can't let go other hand
gripping the blunt letting the
smoke blow, hiting me because
yo boy use to push the snow
pushing them white pillows
you know doing what I gotta do
to real reeling in the dough
you know for show I'm all about
that clash flow making moves like
Bobby Fisha you know when your
gone the police won't miss ya.
Everyday walking to my own death
Loving every breath like it was the
last one. Out here gripping for the
loot protecting my own with the chrome
Ready to shot those Rudy poof
yadada mean. Too fresh on the scene
collecting that mean green fuck stay
dirty I'm too busy staying clean using
digital can't afford a triple beam bitch
I'm a hustla, everyday walk to own death
protecting my head gripping my nut sac
training to catch lead. They put a price on
my head and ain't changed, staying lo key
taking blunt to the brain maintaining my mental
Jumped out the car now I'm heading to the rental
My nigga change the dental, walking to my own death
I can taste last meal and the chill of ice paying the price for living this hard life

*

<u>Staying as low kye</u> as possible hoping they catch im slipping so I'm dipping crossing state lites like the world is mine doing 10 over the speed and everything is fine one hand on the wheel the other hand griping my own chrome with no time to waste

I gotta keep moving looking in the rear view to make no ones pursuing, making fine time doing what I do time to gas up eyes watching me and I don't know who can't stop now homie I thought you knew eyes on the prize trying to stay alive paying the price of living the life stuck in an insane state constantly rolling the dice living this hard life with packs to move and money to make taking penationary chances trying to fill my plate so I'm staying low kye and I know their watching me and if I get caught then it's all on me but I can't stop now waiting to ease the load once I touch down no time to sleep, one hand gripping the wheel and the other hand gripping my heart ain't like grand taking these chances taking risks

THROWING HOOKS
DON'T STEAL MY STUFF BITCH

Burn one for the po one
Smoking blunt after blunt
Riding sky high maintaining my mental
Sitting lo key sliding in a rental
Windows rolled up watching the smoke
Fly around kicking back lo key listening
To the bass pound. Burn one for the
po one

Why don't these bitch
Nigga's understand me
They gotts to die
For fucking with my
Family doing my thang
These niggas can't stand
Me they gotts to die
Don't you understand me

living this hard life it's eat or starve so I ain't gotta think twice it's a day to day gamble living my life sweet as rain or as cold as ice. Keeping my eyes on the road staying in the lane if they catch me now they might split my frame take me out and split my brain living a life that's never fair with no gaurantees just empty promises promised and dreams of getting paid living the good life so I can relax in the shade hoping to live a life with no worries, time to pick up the pace so I can clean my self off living the hard life with no time for soft keeping one hand on the wheel while I put a blunt in the air trying to maintain my mental riding low key never slipping dipping sliding in a rental getting rid of the aroma in the air no time stop I gotta it keep moving I know they watching me you see me moving low key making this everyday gamble paying to price to me life doing what I do taking these penatenery chance riding low key to make my dreams come true with one hand on the wheel and my other hand on my nut sac and the heat under the seat and I'm almost home no time to waste so I slow down lean back and hide my face staying calm and collective I'm almost home time to drop off and clean up a stash the chrome living the life I live paying the price of life with no gaurantees just dream of living the good dodging these felonies.

O and you ain't know out here staying on the grind pushing <u>you know</u>. Out here fighting against these mean streets with my grind face on hustling just to eat in these mean streets all day long doing what it do until it do something else I ain't out here pounding the concreate for my health, in these streets where it's hard to compete out here with my grind face on trying to make ends meet. Fighting to keep my space ready to hit the streets with my game laced. I ain't running from nobody they already know my face out here pounding the concreate keeping my pace fighting in this life of crime until they come and take mine living in these mean streets until they come and take mine out here living under this hot California sunshine. Out here doing for self I got my life on the line out here risking my health keeping it moving playing the cards I was delt. Keeping the dice rolling I ain't running from nobody even when I see them black and whites pattroling holding even when I'm hot holding, never folding under pressure, I'm down for whatever, out here pounding the concreate no matter the weather rain sleet or snow on the grind pushing you know, stacking sky high until I'm rolling in the dough and you should already know I'm staying on the grind because my pockets said so. Out here protecting my space staying laced up at all times, making money in due time. Out here on these mean streets to take whats mine, living in this world of glitts and grime ready to do the time for the crime because it is what is it what it is living the life of pop pop there it is no expenation needed because it is what it is and that's how it is. Out here face to face with the grind I don't know about you but I'm out here to get whats mine face to face with the grind I'll get whats mine in due time until then it's the life of the grind, out here pounding the concreate walking under the hot California sunshine protecting my space. They already know me and memerized my face, out here living a life of grind stuck in the life of crime they ain't giving me shit so I gotta go out and take mine it's either time or crime. When they come to take mine keeping my grind face on to get mine in due time until then I'm stuck in the grind trying to get whats mine pounding the hard concreating grinding in the sunshine they ain't giving me shit so I'm to take mine

What is what it is
It is what it is

Holla at my potna D
Marro for $700+
minor car problems

MAN
Don't you see how
Cruel life can be
When you slide with me
If you ride with me

Everytime I leave the house
I got eyes watching me as soon
I jump into my ride bend the block
and the police follow me
watcthing me trying to catch yo boy
doing bad
Thinking that I'm hot just
because I left the pad
so sad

On probation and they trying
to get me to cross the
invisible state life I stop
talking on the phone so they
tapped my mind

26 years old but I feel
I'm running out of time
If they try to do me in
Then it's the end of my blood line

Thinking to myself
mybe they forgot
to check the pedigree
Getting over on yo boy
it can't be
not me

Smoking that California purple lime
to help ease my mind
Staying low out of sight
Paying warrieness off
So I don't see time

Back against the wall
protecting me, myself and
my family staying strapped

up so my foe's don't damage me
ravenge me now we know
we can't have that when them
hollow tips fly you best to
bug back dig that

In my life all I have
is heart and soul
my dick and two balls
with my hood instincts with the
ambition to ball
I don't have shit to
lose with my back against
the wall

No love for me
Don't write
Don't call
Why you hating on me
When we all suppose to ball
But you know me
I refuse to fall
I'll just kick back
smoke a fat sac
untill my money tall
That how it is in
my day to day life
stacking a grip
avoiding them boys
because I roll the dice

My life is nothing nice
If birds of a feather fly together
Then why am I flying solo

Trying to set me up to wet me up
They <u>framing</u> me charging
for things I didn't do
They're <u>hating</u> me trying to
get the police to pursue
They're <u>blaming</u> me got no
back up that I can do
It's all on me

Ambulance first on the scene
Fireman the reach up the murder scene
Then the police came after
looks like another one
neigherhood dezaster
Police taped off the
street to contain the heat
Watching the coronor bringing the bodies
to the street
Victums wraped up
Wearing cotton bloody sheets
Family on the side line
crying on the street
Now family members missing
Another murder on the street
A murder rap
Another life lost
Protecting the family
And life was the cost
Another chess move
just to become boss
Took them car,
the money and the
product to floss
what a lose
what a shame
for somebody to
split and aim for your brain
for a little piece
of change

Now they're in the public look for the suspect
Said they had leads but they ain't caught none yet
You can see the tears falling from
the faces in the crowd
You can hear the crys over the sirene sounds
Another life lost another head put down
I feel for the family and will never ever forget the sound
Sirenes die down
Now they're asking the family question
if they were in the house
at time their bodies would be streching
Thinking about family friends

Got them all second guessing
All this carnage without no evidence
No suspect and no witnesses found
Nobody around to hear the bullets fly round
How sad to see another murder victum on the street
Another life lost put down by hood heat

This is my life stuck in this hard life
With one life roll the dice and I'm paying the price
Life is a gamble and living on these streets that are cold as ice
I paid the price
These streets will leave you frozen living the hard life following the road that I've chosen
frozen cold as ice, but that life
After you let go, only the dice know
living this life because it's the only life I know
Cold as snow, trying to catch me pushing that snow
Living the only life I know in this world as cold as ice
Living my life rolling the dice gambling paying the price for
living this hard life

Amazing simply blunts blazing feeding the clip watching the hollow tips blazing. Simply amazing blunts blazing just letting the shit fly no lie no evidence and no need for an aliby to tuff for the truf living the hard life kicking back moving work with no time to work bitch I'm doing that block thang letting my sac swang kicking back relaxing letting my nuts hoing letting the shit fly while I fly bye no lie grab the wheel while I bust the steel aimed and ready to eject at will eyes on the prize while I grip that steal don't worry about nothing just grip that wheel, talking to a nigga that was taught to grip that steal. Coming where I'm from where we were built to kill keeping my eyes on the prize just grip that wheel. Too tuff for the turf living a life of pushing work pulling ho cards and pulling up skirts doing this block thang kickback blazing sacs letting my nut hang just relax grip the wheel and let me do my thang simply amazing cockback and unload sit back and watch as the hollows explode, don't let go hold the wheel don't let go pass me the extra clip so I can rip through sending these slugs at him sharper then a gense (grab the wheel) hold on I'm fen to one clip wasn't enough I gotta send two. Simply amazing blunts blazing emptying the clip unloading the magazine letting the hollow tips rip mind over matter watching the brain splatter I'm going in forgotten so the evidence don't matter. Just letting the shit fly no lie no evidence needed and no need for an aliby just letting shit fly smoking pound after pound listening to sound of my gun sray this nigga tried to take mine that's why I'm out here playing with gun play. My mind gone crossed the line trying to take my mind and rip me to pieces, so I bombed unloading semi automatic metalic pieces ready for quick release they tried to take me out so I had to bomb back release the beast. Time to throw away the throw away and the heat got the box waiting let me know when your ready staying toes cocked armed and deadly. Simply amazing

HEAD GONE

Head gone smoking purp mind in a zone drinking that purple and sprite blunts rolled tight stuck to my seat relaxing kicking up my feet. Mind gone that purple got me lifted mixed with that California lime from my California line that moves coast to coast on that California pipe line that always on time wraped up and sent to me living the high life come get high with me smoking that purple drinking purple mixed with gasoline stuck in the zone. Melted to my seat with my head blown putting the blunt to the flame trying to find my way home. Staying lifted I'm gift rolling up the finest one of the first to bring out that purple homie you couldn't find this one of California's finest, staying twisted mind lifted wit my in the zone fuck matching sac for sac I'm talking about matching zones, so come and get high with me, some purple smoke some purp come get high with stuck to my seat with my head in the zone matching. blunt after blunt until the zone's gone with my head blown high as I wantta be gotta live the high life you want to get high with me, drink purple and with my blunts rolled tight matching bottle after war zone for zone my minds blown all night match another homie yeah I might, so get the blunt to the flame let the weed ignight. Drinking purple smoking purple high all night.

Come over here baby and let a grown man seduce you I'm out of the ordinary not the average nigga you used to come over here and holla at a playa is something that you should do I'm not the average joe I'm something you should get used to so come here baby and let this grown man seduce you.

Just come through you know I'll kill it I know nobody will work the middle like I did it so smooth with it kickback relax and just groove with it

(rewrite)

I'm super hard with it I take my strap to the shower I want it all not just a piece of the pie plus about a mill an hour. Let the bullshit slide I'm to dumb for that shit caught me sliding in a all black chevy with a strap to match doing my do dirt in style staying hyphy with it I been in the game for a while just bring me the money I can care less if you like my stlye I'm too busy baby boy out here doing my thing stacking up a grip collecting dollers my nigga doing my thing it ain't enough hours in a day I got just enough in the clip sitting low ready for trigger that how we do it out here playing how playas play you ain't doing it right unless your doing it my way slamming the bass to the sound of gun play (my nigga what you say) don't pay attention to me you better listen to the gun spray staying low kye and out of sight rolling up a blunt trying to find a light creeping times crawling rolling superhand with it hoping these niggas don't make me kill to night if everythings cool these niggas just might survive the nigga no time to worry about these nigga I'm to busy trying to find a light with no haters in sight it's time to get up and get gone with it I just sparked it up so don't ask me to hit it big bosses do more then puff puff passing out here rolling perfecttos wipe off your lips home boy I'm high as fuck I'm might just go if your wet lips start harassing so be quick with it hit that and pass it back pitch in where you sit in yall nigga's got to ain't up before yall get in if not I'll watch yall listening to the tires spin no rest for the whore I'm super hard with it guess yall niggas didn't hear me I want it all not just a piece of the pie I'm high as fuck you know I ain't go lie out here owning the streets high I die what you looking at potna ain't no pussy over here niggas die for less I'm super hard nigga you can't pump fear these niggas out here muggie it must be the haters time of year

Fucking with a deranged psyco servearly loco sitting low key on low pros selling boats and shipping keys if I can't get it around here then I ship from across seas, time to take a trip a g per ship make sure I count it carefully these nigga's known to dip I can't slip I must stay on toes can't nickle and dime now, when you fucking with pros sit back and stack cheese just like I'm suppose if your not a pill popper I got something for the nose can't nickle and dime no more this shit here ain't for show I'm a money motavated hustla I'm in it for the cash flow doing it big like Johnny Depp in blow if you ain't doing it big then what the fuck you doing it for

Rewrite

(empty promises are just words until they become more than words)

Dying is easy living is hard to do when you live the hard life and got the barrels pointed at you living this life where real niggas die too when it's over it's over when your gone there's nothing life can do living my life to the fullest with a grip on the wheel until my life is through when it's over it's over there's nothing life can do living my life to the fullest until my life is through dying in these streets is easy living is hard to do trying to survive in this life where real niggas die too. Living in these mean streets with barrels pointed at you ready to spit at you with no problem to fold you up protecting my space until my time is up. Just me myself and my chrome living my life until they call me home living with my little piece of pistal so I'll never die alone living this hard life paying the price to live life taking blunts to the dome stuck to the grind until my life is gone trying to forget the pressure the stress and the pain trying to maintain sane in a world that remains insane hoping life get love for me expecting the worst and always hoping for the best just another day in the hard live I live trying to stay focused and live the life I live life ain't easy for me death could be waiting around the corner for me I try to stay focused. I don't really trip off too much eyes always on me so I can't really do too much life is hard and niggas die easy I could tell you about my life but you propably wouldn't believe me trying to stay focused hoping my eyes don't decieve me living this hard life where dying is easy living with my little piece of pistal with my ghetto grin living in a world where niggas die for real out here living with these niggas don't pretend they cockback aim and shot to kill that's why I live with my little piece of pistal and my twelve gauge pump ready to dump on these fools leave them slumped eyes wide open swimming in their own pool filled with lead then throw away the throw away then take a blunt to the head living this life ain't easy where niggas die easy I could tell you my life story but you probably wouldn't believe me striaght down dirty grimmie and greasy living this hard life where even the strongest die easy, hoping when I go I don't die for nothing catch me in a storm of bullets with my 45 cocked back busting with my game face on hoping to never die alone hoping they don't catch me slipping naked without my chrome hoping to go out in a blaze of glory with a blunt in my mouth before they turn my lights out then I'm out hoping I didn't die alone living this hard life where niggas die easy I could tell you how I live but you wouldn't believe me trying to stay focused hoping my eyes don't decieve me stuck in the life where niggas live hard and even the strong die easy

Pick up the phone bass off talk on staying clean I don't know if they trapped my phone I already know they tapped my home. Picked up the trying to find out what's on somebody on the move trying to crush groove I'm knowing it's all good I just gotta make moves I'm too clean right now, I can't push and pull hit me in a little minute and everything should be cool, be cool I'm out here running around town, can't talk too much you know how I get down. Put the phone down never knowing who's listening in they might be listing. Staying collective pulling in they know I'm dirty even when I stay clean out here pulling in like a well oiled machine I stay clean riding on the pipe line pulling lines that take time sticking to the streets staying cool calm and collecting keeping mind over muscles pockets out here streaching no time to flex sticking to the streets when it's time to collect. Time to pick up make moves and drive to collect. He hit back to collect crush moving time takes time taking time when I'm moving sticking to streets tuff talking when I'm moving sticking to the groove while I'm sticking the streets I'm on the way out here trying to find the street I'll be there in a little minute come out and find me you know I'm in watch your mouth you never know whos on the trapped my and they might tap my phone eyes watching me listening in sticking to the streets in case they try to close in keep it street just in case they listen in playing it safe in case they try to close in. Stay clean playing in the streets that stay mean I'm still stuck to the

∗ <u>Figure out a plan</u>, to bring a person with no <u>place</u> to <u>live</u>, and <u>no money</u> into an independent working enviorment, shealters, food, and other nessaties included. To a situation were that person owns <u>property</u> or/and <u>business</u>.

∗ Some kind of <u>temporary</u> <u>service</u>, with <u>shealters</u> and <u>dependable</u> <u>transportation setting goals</u>, saving money and then after gaining experience in the work force start a career or business taking baby steps to meet the goals.

streets driving on the pipe line taking time doing shit that takes time sticking to the streets waiting for collect time still out here waiting in these mean streets taking time for taking mine so come meet me in the streets time to pick up I'm here sticking to the streets. Don't call me again I told you come find me in the streets, I'm here then I'm gone sticking to the groove back to the pipe line living in these streets where they tap and watch mine. Sticking to the streets stuck in the groove to collect mine stuck in these mean street sticking to the groove so they can't take mine staying on, on my phone until they need some next time.

When I'm just trying to maintain with this life of stress and strain and madness on my brain living with the bullshit of life when I ready paid the price for rolling the dice. Just trying to stand tall before they set me up and create me to fall walking away from the bullshit wading through it all. Living in a world where it's them against me in this world where they hate me from me for being me. Just trying to stand tall before I fall into the depts, trying to hold on to my life as I step every step, wading through the bullshit, gripping on to my own walking away from the bullshit trying to let go. I already paid the price waking away from the bullshit holding on to my life I' already paid the price for rolling the dice, walking away from the bullshit out here living my life. I trying to hold on to the life that I have left walking away from the bullshit step bye step. Living in the world surround by hate where it's them against me. Walking away from the bullshit just trying to be me in this world where they hate me for being me. Trying to separate my self from the bullshit that follows me, living with the stress and strain of the world where it's them against me, trying to walk away from the bullshit that follows me. Walking away from the bullshit trying to let go of the hate that follow me. Living in this world where it's them against me.

STANDING ON MY OWN TWO

No time for the bullshit I gotta pick on my own two and stay strong separating myself from hate and now it's time to move on and the bullshit move on. I gotta stay strong and let the hate slide bye standing on my own two watching time roll bye separting myself from the bullshit that seems to follow me living in a world where it's them against me trying to live my life and stop the bullshit from trapping me. I gotta move on and stay strong through it all separating myself from hate trying to stand tall. Not knowing the outcome wading through it all living this life where it's them against me, living a life where I was born to fall. No time for the bullshit separating myself from hate in a world where it's them against me trying to stand tall while they hate me for being me living in a world where me is the only way to be, walking away from the bullshit that follows me in this world where hate surrounds me, living this life where it's them against me. I'm trying to move on and stay strong walking through life with my head up, with some much stress and strain on me. It's hard for me to get up, living in this world where enough isn't enough, and I'm trying to stand tall and keep moving leaving the bullshit behind standing on my own two living to the beat of mine hoping to get back on my get back in no time standing on my own two living this life of mine. I'm trying to stay strong pushing the hate aside even though the bullshit seems to follow me in this world filled with hate living a life where it's them against me, where the hate of the world surrounds me, caught up in the stress and strains the drowns me trying to walk away but the bullshit seems to follow me. I'm trying to stay strong and walk away but they pull me back me, setting me up to lose when I'm out here trying to win, as soon as I make it out of the game they pull me back in. Trying to maintain living with this bullshit stress and strain, trying to stay dry while they keep me in the rain

Fuck these punk motherfuckers out here talking shit bitch nigga I ain't going now I standing right here bitch so let's do what it do I don't give a fuck I'm standing right here I ain't no motherfucking punk so jump jump bitch nigga we can get it right now we can take it to the street or stand face to face and bust rounds bitch nigga I'm here standing on my own two standing right here so bitch nigga jump if you want too, you know I get something for them ass I don't give a fuck so bitch nigga jump jump fake bitch made switching motherfucker doing nothing but talking shit when right bring it straight to you bitch so man up bitch nigga and stop talking shit you punk bitch I'm standing here standing on own two and I ain't going nowhere don't give a fuck yall bitch made nigga I ain't going nowhere if you something potna then man up I'm not scared I'm standing right here potna I never bitch up and run scared I'm ain't going no where bitch nigga I'm standing on own two right here so jump if you wanta bitch nigga I never gave a fuck so quit talking shit bitch nigga and run up ain't no fear on mind standing on my own two protecting mine talking shit behind my back bitch nigga I'm standing right here so do what it does bitch nigga I ain't going no where standing on my own two so man up I ain't scared of shit so bitch nigga jump. I'm standing right here willing and waiting it's just you and potna I'm standing and wanting you ain't pumping no fear you just pumping you lips bitch nigga when I'm standing right here showing no fear so man up bitch nigga I'm wanting right here you ain't wanting for me because I'm standing right here never giving a fuck so bitch nigga jump fuck these bitch made nigga and these motherfucking punks we can go glock for glock bitch nigga shot for shot fucking with a nigga harder the crack rocks ready to lift you out seat bitch nigga and take you out your socks loaded up and ready to go glock for glock bitch nigga I'm standing right here I ain't scared of shit and I ain't running no where. Toe to toe bitch nigga it's just you and me I'm waiting on you, you ain't got to wait on me bitch nigga I ain't going no where bitch nigga I'm standing right here so bitch nigga piece up or shut the fuck up and give me my space I'm standing right here potna staring at this bitch nigga face to face with no fear on mine ready to take mine so man up bitch nigga and stop wasting my time sick of these bitch made motherfuckas hating on mine so give what's mine before I come and take mine

Finish this one

I'm yo hit man for hire, pull out cockback then squeeze to fire, there ain't no faking the funk, we dope boys out here as long as the cash is right you get want you want, we will and they won't, I can fill the bag as long as there's room in the trunk, let me introduce you to Mr. Moss Berg pump let off squeeze then dump. Bitch I'm a killa how would you like the taste off saw off gunpowder to the face, leave you wit a hole in yo head with that sweat after taste bitch I'm a killa, yo hit man for hire. Riding to the sound of automatic fire, nigga no need to seise fire I'm yo hit man for hire

12-24-09

A pretty lady
You drive me crazy
I think I love you
I would do anything for you

12-25-09

itcha itcha itcha gotta ya
who droped ya
who did you bad man
itcha, itcha itcha gotta ya
who shot ya
who did you bad man
itcha, itcha itcha gotta ya
who popped ya who did you bad man
itcha itcha pop itcha itcha pop

I'm hella high a a a
I'm hella high a a a a
I hella high
I'm hella high a a a a

[Hook]   12-22-09

I got thirty two dollas and a nickle sac
I got thirty two dollas and a nickle sac
I got thirty two dollas and a nickle sac
I got thirty two dollas and a nickle sac

who shot ya who droped ya
a nigga ran up and popped ya
who shot ya who droped ya
that's what you get for fucking
with a mobsta
who shot ya who droped ya
a nigga ran up and popped ya
who that's what ya get for
fucking wit a mobsta
that's what you get for fucking
with a mobsta that's what you get for fucking wit a mobsta

Don't you see the Angels cry for me, rolling up blunt after blunt watching these blunts live just to die for me, anything can happen when you ride with me sip, dip, and slide with me, drowning in weed smoke watching the Angels cry for me, crused to live life, wishing I could live twice a double up on life, and watch these haters fly bye stuck to the grind getting mine a hundred dolla bill at a time, try living a black mans life without a hustle or grind, sticking to the game plan and never change up, when my trigger gets tired that's when I change up you can see the pain in the faces that surround me, I thank GOD for the grind, the Angels and all, stacking money to the sky and I'm always high gotta be careful out here they cut niggas wing off when they try to fly just stick to recipe and watch the dough roll in beware hata of this lighting I'm holding, my aim is golden but my shot is priceless, watching the Angels cry for me, because they can't sin for me, but momma I gotta get it, even if the Man up stairs ain't down with it, it's so cold out here, niggas straped up so bold out here, but they can't pump fear, that soft nigga you think I am, ain't here, Momma I push soft and I thank GOD for the loot, counting my blessing daily, the nigga pulled out but thank GOD he didn't shoot, I didn't understand why Angels cry for me, but now I see, they smell the sin that surrounds me Angels sitting on my shoulders and I can't brush them off, taking in the Good and the BAD I want it all I been high half my life I'm fly to high to fall, and tell the Devil I ain't MAD at all, temptation brings profit, they called for a neutral profit and homie I'm it, you can see the future in every ryhme I spit you can tell the real from the fake from every hand shake you get it's all about money now life and death ain't shit, trapped in this world that let's sin surround me. I was lost until the pen found me, them other niggas tried to down, them boys tried to drown me and my connect cut me off, but them true GO gettas shot me love fuck them hating nigga because a grown man can't leave on crumbs, I stay hungry out here addicted to the life, I just hope that my soul ain't the prize for life, watching the Angels cry for me but I can't cry they can't die for me, turn the beat up and listen to the Angels cry for me, watching the smoke bounce off the window as the blunts continue to die for me listening to the Angel's cry

Why me why me why me why

[Yes it's me being as real as I can be just follow yo nose if ever want to find me. I'm one of a kind fresh and genuine. Stacking every dolla I find fuck these fake motherfuckas the world is mine]

All I see is dollas everytime, floating on weed smoke swimming in gin tell the Man up stairs I'm all in doing what I do best. It's the top and nothing less mind over muscle living my life if GOD bless and yes I smoke weed, yes I stay keed, yes. I stack racks to help water my seed. I'm a new breed, the last of the realest, so I know you feel me, and I got something hot and heavy for them hustas trying to kill me, stick to my nine my money and my loot I can give a fuck about these hater niggas pointing my chevy. I don't give a fuck about you nigga I'm riding heavy so show what you know. I got fade my nigga and pounds to blow. How many clips does it take to fill you up, have that nine deal you up, these niggas dead and gone. Like a blunt to the dome, you better listen to yo gut or catch a clip to the bottom, no evidence needed Officer I shot him, and remember you heard it from me, out here keeping my eyes open and my ear to the street, I can't fuck with these niggas who miss the beat I'm the nigga locked and loaded gripping the heat, barbquing every nigga I meet, cutting in to these niggas like a gensue to raw meat, nigga I'm it unloading the fire I spit the best is what I want, so the real is ALL I get, the realest nigga I know out here. Killing shit marking down every top notch bitch I hit, homeboy yo bitch is taken, coming up and out yo bitch while you at home waiting, nigga yo bitch is taken just applie game and the mind earses, mo money, mo hos, and mo cases. That's all I know stuck to the grind for all time, watching the smoke blow, and I got it for the low, coming up out yo bitch but she still got miles to go, moving P's to pounds of snow; ball to you fall, then climb back up. Enough may be enough for you, but to me enough is never enough. Stacking every dolla I find the world is mine.

Cold in these streets I can't afford a heart, starting from scratch riding low kye in back of the lac, these niggas screaming murder and I glad I heard ya. Keep eyes in the back of yo head, we all bleed red. Creaping up on these bitch made niggas delivering a clip to the head, it's cold out here and I show no fear, griping my stack and my nut sac because my nine on my lap, they fucking with these niggas, and these niggas will leave yo head on flat, I'm the shooter and the gettaway driver nigga I'm a rida rida doing what ridas do, if it's time to get down wit the get down then my nigga slide through, and bring yo mask wit ya I'm jumping in my car now nigga only a real nigga will ride wit ya, die wit ya, sip, dip and slide wit ya no mo talk I'm wit ya

TO FIND THE KEY

An empty life, a worthless world where nothing seems to make cents, everything is meaningless and promises remain empty what world is this, and why did life send me. I wonder if death will avenge me and put an end to life and it's meaninglessness leaving me with peace and quite, with no worries to worry and no problems to take care of, living an empty life with hardly any help from above, and so much hate here below the skyline cursed with life, living this life of mine, I guess even dying takes time, living in this worthless world with this empty life of mine. Nothing remains the same, everything is upside down, crisscrossed and constantly rearranged, living in this empty world were only time has changed. Everything empty and hollow living in this empty worthless world with so much sarrow, and nothing makes cents, no cents at all even with all the answers the world continues to fall, everything to gain and everything to loose, living in this worthless world with only death to choose with constant reminders that life won't win, I can't win, life let's death choose the fate of the living. For the sake of fun and games, or is it for the sake of living, where even fact seems like fiction and open doors stay shut, and life is death feeling the voice of death in every breath reminding me, life can't last forever, but death will last for an eternity, leaving me with nothing with nothing but an empty vessel, with no life for me. This worthless world was never meant for me, living beneath the skyline with no help from above for me. Nothing seems to make cents, and after a while nothing seems to matter, there is just time and space and vessels waiting to become empty. Living in this empty world a worthless existence living the life, that life sent me so quick, always ready to leave so fast, seems the only way to find meaning in life is through death, the reaper waiting for me to pass and pass on, I wonder why we even bother to hold on, the strong become weak the become strong, then life waits for death waiting for the weak to pass on. I guess only the strong will survive until life becomes death. Is life only what life leaves behind or is it just another piece to the puzzle and link in the chain under the skyline, just another part of the timeline. Such an empty life I live, even though I live, where did the meaning go, and where did life take me, am I just living to die, waiting for death to take me, will the open doors stay shut, or will they stay open for me, I was told, I was promised that I wouldn't need a key to enter. I was told I had a place waiting for me, I was told it wouldn't take thought and I was the key, living this life I live, the life that life sent me, living under the skyline, while the touch of death tempts me, will I pass, and pass on and walk through the gates that should remain open for me, I was told to live my life and I already hold to key.

THE REAPER

I can feel the reaper closing in, the one who holds no remorse for life. The one who gives no mercy, always ready, and willing, to take what eventually belongs to death the reaper I can feel the presence of death in every movement, every moment, and every breath I take. I can here the reaper calling, but I don't know if, I'm ready to meet my fate. Feeling the tempeture drop as my body starts to cool and turn knumb, my body starts to shake I can feel my bones sheiver and rattle like the tail of a poisonos snake, warning passerby, letting it be known that death is close by. I get cold sweats, and I feel so cold, is this what you're suppose to happen when your body grows old, I'm not ready to go. I can remember it like yesturday when I bought my first piece of bubble gum, has time crept up and caught up with me, has it been that the one that has always been there for me turns out to be the one that puts the end to me. Life is almost over and the reaper has sent for me, my body is ready to go but my mind is not made up, the reaper is coming for me, and I have a life that I'm not ready to give up. I can't just give up, there most be something I can do, something I can say to, pay the toll for life and make the reaper go away. Is my life the only price the reaper will except. Is there something I do to persuade the reaper to keep him away when death calls, persuade the one who holds no remorse, the one who gives no mercy, the one who doesn't discremanate, the one that takes all, the one who takes life when death calls. I can feel him closing in, I can feel death watching me, the reaper's close, breathing, the reapers breath cooling off my skin. Fighting a losing battle I can't win. Fighting a fight with the reaper, and I know I won't win, where did my life go, how did time pass so quickly. Life is so brief, gone so fast, here today gone tomorrow, watching the sands pass through the hour glass of time that I have left holding so closly to every moment, every breath. Now it's only me and time search for life that I can't seem to find. I can see the reaper closing in to take the life of mine. I hope when the reaper takes my hand, and takes the life of my mine, I'll be fine. If I could just hold on the the memories of mine, don't worry about life even dying takes ???

This clip for you - you know how I do, fuck me then fuck you
This clip here's for you

I excepted defeat along time ago wrapped up in a whirlwind, riding with my nine at all time, my life ain't nothing nice, niggas shooting and blasting all about my paper and my money my cash and I don't give a fuck about these haters when I'm blasting, I do what my clip tell me to do. Fuck a hata man I got shot better then you hoping my T-shirt don't get wetter then you, pockets to the brim and my pedal to the floor, sticking to the grind nigga get what you asked for, got that my money running in my blood and I'm itching and blasting. I don't give a fuck about a hata man I'm all about my cashin. All straped from back to back. I'm a real hood nigga man, I don't know how to act, I got a itchy trigga finger you can run and tell em that, itching and blasting, give a fuck what a hater say I'm all about my cashin I'm out here on the grind standing on my own two. I could give a fuck about a bitch made nigga this clip for you. This clip for you - you know how I do fuck me then fuck you

This clip here's for you

CASH FIRST I RECUPERATE THIS

CAPACORN CAPIN

Another day in the life
Another day, another price
Hustling making that money rollin
wrist shining like ice pushing
that hard shit living the hard life.

Living my life alwayz caught between a rock and a hard place only the real can relate shaking the fake off and getting gone if you'll if don't want to piece up then I'll get it my own, go and get it myself and sell my own. To me it just another day in the life paying the price living the life of a everyday hustla. If you fake I can't trust ya, let the hollows its rust you, and put you deep down, where I can trust ya where I'm from potna real hustlas don't play around, we spit round for round laying bitch nigga down, how does that sound. Fake niggas get no love for me, just put the money in my hand you can touch my OZ. I'm a OAKLAND smoking OG. My product not for free cash first homie you know me. Just another day in the life of a Hustla trying my best to do my thug thang kick back roll up a fat sac and let my nuts hang. Just another day, another price. Just another day living a hustlas life

AMAZING

Simply amazing blunt blazing feeding the clip watching the hollow tips blazing. Simply amazing; blunts blazing just letting the shit fly no lie no evidence and no need for an aliby to ruff for the turf nothing to do but kickback and move work, no time to work bitch I'm doing that thang kicking back relaxing bitch letting my money back hang bitch doing my thang making money, moving work. Bitch doing what I gotta do to push. it's simply amazing cockback and unloaded watching the hollow tips blaze up hollows in the nine fit in the AK so bitch blaze up it's simply amazing pound for pound blunt blazing pass me the clip and I'm blazing grab the wheel busting bitch out here hot as I wanta be not taking shit nobody heat up or cool off the block like me simply amazing nina cockback armed and ready press aim so deadly while I'm blunt blazing shit bitch nigga I'm just simply amazing

My mind gone, cross that line and I'll take your mind get your mind ripped to piece dealing with a nigga that's one of a kind selling ho no leases fully metal jacket with semi auto metalic pieces ready for quick release bitch nigga time to release the beast bitch catch heat fall stand fully armed.

Fuck the dumb shit put the bullshit to the side and piece up and watch the money roll in. Do this shit for real never pretend play the game and and I was play to win, know the rules to the game and stay on your toes at all times, protect self no time for beef, but keep my nina next to me for these bitch nigga's who pretend away to creap. Playing to win I can't afford to lose living life with nothing to prove sticking the grove it stacking money all day staying in the groove. Less problems mean no money for me. More money for us with guns we bust, for money we lust. You can have my bitch I got the lootche and fuck another bitch cochie I don't give a fuck. Lets get this dough. If you don't want to get it for yourself, then do it for the dough. Keep it stacking watching the blunts blow. Moving everything for green to that all white snow staying money motavated. Kicking it with money makers and hoe takers, and fake shakers. Don't hate on me, I'll det that nina nine ease your mind. Remember homie boy grinding takes time and right now the world is mine. Sticking with me and mines getting it all day on the grind, making money the hard way doing it for the loot, the grip and the shine the world is mine.

Bring it in

Cook it up and send it out, making this loot is what it's all about. Gain respect collect loot than I'm out the hustla on the block that. Time to cool whistling talking was off take a vacation and let my nuts hang. Than back to the block to do my thang. Doing it for the real nigga's and bitches who do their block thang, turf talking letting them nut swang. While I put blunts in the mind collecting dollers doing my thang. Now back to the block to do that money thanga kick back relax on the block and <u>let my nut swang</u> letting that money roll in just doing my thang if you knew what I mean

Fuck those who choose to have no love for me
Do anything in they're power to hate on me
Fuck them all ALL bullshit to the side potna

I'm out to ball stacking my loot, grip standing tall. Climbing to the top I can't fall, it's too late for that. Picked the dope game to bring in that scratch, like that bring it in and watch that money bank stack making so much money. I don't know how to act so I make a grip sit back and watch my money stack. Racking in with due progress. Life in the dope game making progress. No second guessing. No fake niggas trying to flex get touched by the tech, hit filled from toe to kneck. Fuck those who choose to have no love for me. Doing anything in their power just to hate on me. Smile in my face and then fake on me. Why don't they see I'm not the one to fuck with. Pick up my chrome lady and let the hollows spit. I'm sick, bitch nigga don't test my nuts know real killa, who will leave your body in the back of a pick up. When it's time to clean up. Another day in the life. Playing in the dope game where real niggas get slain and caught up in prosuit for the loot. Never affraid to stop and shoot. Fuck those who choose have no love for me

Fuck them hating ass niggas and them punk ass Rudy poo's keep my nina next to me ready to shoot. Bitch niggas quit hating on me I'm no phony. I throw the dogs up if you want funk homie. If your better with the fist to cuffs homie than show me. Have no problems taking it to street. One man standing the other met defeat. Nigga don't fuck me fuck those who have no love for me. Them niggas that would do anything just to hate on me. Fuck those bitch made niggas fuck them fuck them all. They all phony bitch nigga don't fake the funk I see your itchy trigger finger ready to bust, for the lust of the loot. Fast cars, and hoes shaking off these Rudy poots kicking with the real with steal ready to shoot.

Hustling

Doing my thang and they froze my account. Now it's time to turn the heat up. Stack my chips to the sky, now I can put my feet up. I bring food to the table, now it's time to eat up, and when product runs low then it's time to re-up. I can't stop untill I reach the top. Now you know I ain't falling. Too close to the top now, so I keep balling. Kickback sitback, and relax and watch my raise to success, for my self I expect the best and nothing less. In this game called life you can either win or loose. I'm a winner because I choose. I keep my money in a safe place in a safe safe. Doing it big, I keep my second stash in the banks safe. Can't do business unless your trust worthy. If I don't trust you can get shit from me. I stay balling homie for those who don't know me. Shaking them suckcus that stay phony. Regardless I make mine finger ready and willing those who want to take mine. I can't stop, I'm too close to the top that's why these haters hate me non-stop. I keep that hardcore coming non-stop. Good to the last drop, I can smell the top. Hate on me now and my nina will pop, and once she starts she don't stop. Bringing everybody with me weather you like it or not.

Cruel Life

Can't you see how cruel life can be if you ride with me. Living the hard life when you slide with me. I guess staying on the grind is the life for me the only way to make it out is to hustla and now I see I guess staying on the grind is the life for me. Jump in the ride and I'll show you how cruel life can be. If you grind with me

Living the hard life, the life of a hustla and got them eyes on me, everyday they try to set me up to catch me slipping and pen it all on me, you see it's just another day to me no sleep for the hustlas out here, I gotta stay on toes constantly chosing between who friend and whos foe, living the hard life and paying the price to hustla always remember to keep your mind over muscle, ready to defend my space if they catch me slipping out here they might take my face while I'm protecting my space living in the world with no love for me just dope sac and cadillac's and mean mugs shoulder shrugs and family with no love for me, living a hard life and paying the price this life is nothing nice out here police keep an eye out, so dope dealers beware but there bigger fish then the police out here. Keep your grip on you at all time living this life with no trust. Keep the stash in a safe in a safe place and protect yours. Keep an eye out no sleeping out here protect yourself at all times these haters out here will do anything to shine, living this hard life and staying on the grind hustling doing my thing from coast to coast out here it's the hustlas that snitch the most.

the seat is a semi automatic not for me I gave it to you I knew they out here plotting on me, trying to catch me slapping and take me out of the game stuck in world that remains insane. Guard your brain and your body with these hollow tips, load up and cockback and let the hollows rip through, check under the seat again and take the other clip too. I'm not doing this for me I'm doing this for you I'm trying to show you how to get down you know how I do. No time for the weak on the streets everybody keep strapps to protect their life living on these streets. If catch a case and I'll be out in less then ten with money to spend, unless they steal from me and put my ass back me. I guess staying on the grind hustling is the life for me living owning these streets, watching how cruel life can be. Do this for yourself and make sure it's never for me. I'm doing what I do because it's all I see living a hard life with no love for me living the hard life and paying the price never knowing the outcome when I roll the dice. The day might be as sweat as rain or a hard as ice out here hustling paying the price just to live life. Now you see how cruel living this hard life can be, living a life with no love for me. Watch out for these hand me down hos who only love the dough quick to set a nigga up sticking to the niggas who push that snow. Living this hard life ain't shit fair that way I put the blunt to the flame and put the weed in the air, paying the price to live this hard life letting you know how cruel this life can be when you push,. Dope dealing on these streets with no love for me, and these niggas that kill for the dough.

Yeah <u>you can have my bitch</u> rub her down fill her up I hope she loves that shit I don't give a fuck you can have that bitch no love losed here homie let it do what it do I just pick up another one and do how I do hope you wear a jimmy better yet wear two I'm sure she'll do the same thing to you better yet I hope that bitch falls in love with you have two and half kids and merrys you. I can't hate the game but I can both hate that bitch sick of the bitch trying to get over, and take my shit, yeah you can have that bitch hope she serves you right I know she'll swallow it. Let her swallow it down and don't forget to get your nuts licked fuck her homieboy you can have that bitch I don't own her shit you can keep that bitch put her in the pocket if you want two. She don't love me but I know she'll fuck you, I hope she loves that shit keep her in the pocket and take all her shit, big ones in her mouth I know she'll swallow your shit when she's with you she can't take my shit yeah homeboy you can have that bitch tattoo your name on that bitch and brand that, shit I don't give a fuck you can have that bitch, no love losed her I'm just doing my thang let that bitch gabble dick until your nuts ring shit if I was you homie I probably do the same thing, bro's over hos unless that bitch likes to ride the dick I hope you bust in her eye I really don't give a shit. Shit you forgot buy maganums, you can use my shit. It ain't my bitch so I don't give a shit. She ain't got no love for me, she don't do shit but fuck me so she must be in heat so do what you do potna to make ends meet. You can have that bitch let her swallow you whole after she swallow meat she doesn't belong to me so it really doesn't matter to me yeah homie you can have that bitch I she sucks you up right with a healthy appetiate I don't give a fuck that bitch ain't my wife you can have that bitch. Keep her for the rest of your life I don't give a fuck that bitch ain't my wife you can have that bitch.

Who holds the lock and key to the city I'm out here hustling all day homie that man is me. Getting it while the getting in good, like I should. Doing it for the money makers, and the dope dealers who rep the hood like they should. Holding the key to the lock pushing keys and OZs, hustling like making money a disease. Neighborhood go getter hoe splitter getting mine every time, keeping that money on my mind. Living the life of shile stacking loot this world is mine built for my kind. Keep weed in the air so I don't blow my mind, calm and focused pushing the dopest to get ahead. Hating ass nigga break bread or catch lead, won't say it again unless you catch lead bitch nigga. No time to keep hate on my head, stick to the game plan, and stack bread and get head from these gold digging ass bitch in the game to take riches from the real, sit back bitch chill you should already know the deal, living with looks that kill and a nine that will, with a itchy trigger finger ready to blast for life and cash. In this game bitch nigga's don't last they get pasted by the real you and I

Chocking on that chocolate tie smoking blunt after blunt. If you smoke I'll fuck your lungs up. Nigga roll up who holds the key to the city rounding up all the real nigga yall coming with me. Fuck them fake motherfuckers if they want me than they'll have to come get me. And catch me with a fully loaded pump bitch nigga to fuck your ass up bitch nigga who holds the lock and key if it's not my nigga homie than it's me nigga.

(2)

Built for a world that wasn't built for me from begining to the end I was set up to lose living this hard life broken battered and bruised on my own I done did it crossed state line are you down with it financally fit if you don't like me you can still suck my dick doing what I gotta do to make ends meet doing what I do putting it out there on the streets hating your boy because I don't leave the house without my heat, all on my own out here with my semi automatic protection keeping my mind over muscle and semi automatic weapon to protect me and mines these niggas here everytime trying to get theirs while they hate on mine. Fuck you give me mines nigga I'm keeping what's my built for a world that wasn't built for me filled with haters at always hate on me asked for help and now hands were lent to me built for a world with no love for me. So I'm out here on my own tooting my chrome watching out for these punk motherfucker trying to following me home and take what I own keeping my nive cocked in case I gotta send that ass home I be dame if I let them catch me slipping out here so I keep a fully load clip you and your head can share built for a world that wasn't built for me and I don't care.

Fuck you nigga I'd rather put a blunt in the air

<u>Nothing fair in love and war</u>, these people will eat your soul just to even the score, taking food out of open mouths and snatch dollers out of pockets just to get ahead stepping on people trying to maintain we no love no room to grow in this world of push and shove living in a world of stress and heart acke and heart break, up rooting me before I can plant my steak searching for an opening in this world of no space dieing to get out before my heart breaks trying to eat up before they snatch my plate. It's hard to sit back and find myself living in this world with the cards I was delt trying to find my home stuck in this busy world trying to find home. Searching for release and a piece of the pie living in this busy world with no room to fly, living in a world where only came about self stepping on the little man before the little man can stand I can't stand living in a world I can't stand living with these people who really don't give a dame, watching the time drift away like hour glass sand living in a world with people I can't stand, taking my legs from under me before I can stand. I'm just trying to stand on my own two just like everybody else when body else thinks helping is bad for health while I'm just living in this world playing the hand I was delt, trying to fill my plate living in a world where people were born to hate just head acke, heart acke, and heart break trying to stand tall in this world of hate. Living in this world of push and shove with no give just take, living in this busy world trying to fill my plate before it's too late living in this world of hate.

Haters hate, the real appreshate, and shake the fake, doing what niggas do. Playing how playas play, living a hard life making money the hard way. Trying not to fall off boy I'm not soft. I'm a hustla's. Catch me smoking everyday, making money roll in smoking pack after pack. Lot the neigborhood sprung, now they don't know how to act. Bring them in break them down and send them out pack after pack. Stacking that loot is what its all about. Living in life that's not free so being a hustla now a days is the only way to be. Money makes the world go round. Shh my nigga don't tell them you got it from me. I don't talk, I can't hear, and my nigga you know I can't see. Real for me is the only way to be. Shaking these fake niggas, off of me, these bitch niggas don't know. They niggas owe me when a nigga doing good the smile in your face, as soon as I turn your back they try to steal off my plate keep my nina next to me I hope yall can relate. Shake the fake and kick it with the real.

Money makers stacking doller bills. Don't do it for fake. My nigga do it for real. I need a million dollers not a million doller deal, my nigga that's real. Keeping my gaurd up for these niggas that shoot to kill, I'm a gansta homie for these niggas that don't know me I don't front and these bitch niggas owe me kick it with the real never the fake that's what the cards showed me. Time to collect what these niggas owe me and that real living in a life where niggas shot to kill. Time to let them know I'm so real, I need a million dollers fuck a million doller deal, living in a life where niggas shot to kill. You can keep the hate bitch nigga I'm in it for the skrill separating the real from the fake protecting mines with my steal in it for the money and the dough so I can count my skrill.

* <u>Publish poem</u>

Call aunty to locate publisher or look on the internet or other information to due with publishing

JUST SITTING HERE

<u>Sitting</u> here in the mist of nothingness
Waiting for a <u>REASON</u> to <u>change</u> <u>seasons</u>.
<u>Watching</u> the <u>reflection</u> in the distance

Wandering if the one I see is a part of me, or does this one just look like me. Sitting here in the mist of <u>nothingness</u>. Living in silence with nothing, but the <u>beat</u> of my own, so cold, so here on my own. No one to talk to, living with no place of my own. Just a lonly man searching for home. Sitting here in the mist of nothingness. Just me, myself, the <u>Ghost</u> and the <u>Darkness</u>. How do I live a life like this. Sitting alone with <u>Love</u> <u>missed</u>. Just sitting here in the mist of nothingness. It's we I miss. No where to go there's no place to belong too. I wonder <u>if they'll miss me</u> when I'm gone too.

(1)
THIS WORLD WASN'T BUILT FOR ME

How can I succeed in this world when I was built to lose living a life that's never fair get caught up hand cuffed and arrested for putting weed in the air living this hard life and paying the price in a world as cold as ice a world filled with head splitters, killas, dope deals, back stabbers, snitches and these fake motherfuckers that steal from me built for a world that wasn't built for me. I was built to lose broken battered and bruised all at the same time trying to stack up while these niggas take mine this bullshit happens everytime living in a world with no love for me but I can't stop now I can't let this bullshit stop me not me I'm too close to. Now fuck these hating ass niggas I won't bow down these niggas ain't better then me if they were they would've steal off my plate living with these niggas that was born to hate I can't for the stress to let go shake these haters off and collect my dough without getting caught up and put down doing my thang representing funk town yeah I love that sound paying the price to live this hard life these niggas soft as rain and I'm as cold as ice.

A big boss. A true hust. A real playa dipped in the sauce. Living the high life. Living for the moment never second guessing life. Living the high life and I'm paying the price. Doing my thang out here hustling rolling the dice of life. Out here in these cold streets cold as ice. If you going to do it, might as well do it big, large and incharge. Doing what I do best making money roll in, and taking chronic to the kneck. Fuck living check to check I gotta get it while the gettings good. Doing what I got to do. Just to make it understood I represent my hood. The Big O funk town all day you ain't doing it right if it not the town way. Fuck them all, and stack tall is what I say. Living in these cold streets where niggas get put down by gunplay. Laught in the crossfire from bullet stray. But I'm a boss, I stay dipped in the sauce if your bitch don't want me then you know it's her lost. I'm boss a true haust playing how true playas plays. If you want done right then do it the right way bossing up living life the hard way living the high life so you know what I pay.

Zip for zip my nigga pound for pound pushing O-shit doing what we gotta do to get that grip no snitching out here so zip yo lips out here. Making boss moves a true house out here melting shit down making moves out here all the way from the deep east to funk town all the way to Jack London Square, taking trips flying sky high staying finacally fit and I think you know why making boss moves because I chose sticking to the game plan so you know I can't lose playing in the major leagues no time for minors you got to be financally fit before I can sign ya throwing hardballs from state to state making boss moves to fill up my plate I gotta eat out here, eyes always watching so hustlas beware keep your eyes and ears open and your mouth wide shut homie you gotta live bye the game plan no snitching allowed snitches don't last long out here they always get put down you know how we get down moving zip for zip slanging pound for pound making boss moves home representing the Big O my nigga forever funk town.

REWRITE
FIX THESE ONE

I'm the one watching the one, watching the one who watches you. The one you can trust one that can make your ass fall, or make all your dreams come true. Here to help you walk through. If you plot on me then you'll fall. Stick with me and I'll show you how to ball. How to get it and stand tall. I can't tell. I must show, watching blunts blow pushing down these haters like domino's. I'm been here holding the hands of time. If you don't understand I can rewind. I win everytime stick with me and we can run this. Living the life. Roll the dice of life without paying the price. I was there to help save your life, you were standing too close to the edge becare watch out for the up haters will try to hold you down. Holding you down just come around. Money comes around the fake claiming to be real. Smile in your face and stab you in the back just ask how does that feel. Stick with me and we can rule the tides. Set the new standard fall down just to climb up, can't give up. Only one way up stick with me it's the only way to be stick with the real. The fake don't know me.

If your real you'll have to show me. I just listen to the things you told me. Real reconize real is what this game showed me. Listen to your heart is what the cards showed me. While I'm the one watching the ones watching the ones who watch you. Ride with me and watch your dreams come true. Nothing in life is fair be careful when you roll the dice, keep your eyes open when you live the hard life one way or the other you'll have to pay the price life can be sweat as rain or as hard as ice remember these street ain't safe when you live the hard life. These streets ain't fair, pay the price to roll the dice to live the hard life if you dare.

HOOK

What do yall motherfuckers want from me trying to push me out the game. Laced my sac because I take blunts to the brain. Doing what I gotta do to stay on top one way non-stop. So what do yall motherfuckers want from me trying to push me out the game and take my brain out the frame that's the reason why I take blunts to the brain. What do yall motherfuckers want from me, talking all this shit and don't know me. So many haters in the game and now I see, yall niggas can't get shit from me.

This is my gun, my protection against the enemy. This is my weapon used to serve me in my time of need. To save my life and the lives of others, built to defend me and the lives of others. I must use my gun to put your lives in jeopardy. These gun we aim and shot for fun we keep the hammers clockback and unload untill the jobs done. This is my gun, use to protect cocked and loaded ready to sever your kneck this my gun, used to kill the enemy so stop tripping home boy and stop grilling me this is my gun.

GOTTA STAY GROUNDED
(1)

Gotta stay grounded living this hard life hoping life has something great in store for me trying not to get caught up in the glitts and glamor of it all, a fansy thing designer cloths and these diamond rings paying the price to live life trying not to get caught up in it all with the weight of the world on my shoulder trying to remain tall, trying to see though all the bullshit trying to stay out of the pullpit, hoping life has something great in store for me living this hard life with all this weight on me. Living a life with no garuntees just potenial falonies, money, designer cloths and fansy diamond rings, living this hard life hoping to remain the same keeping my head up taking blunts to the brain just to maintain trying to stay grounded and focused at all times trying to keep the bullshit out, and let the weed cloud my mind. Trying to stay grounded taking one step at a time trying my best to relax and let the weed cloud my mind, taking the world in one step at a time, trying to stay grounded and protect my mind.

(hook on the front of the previous page)

• What you hating niggas wanta do. I can be a nigga to <u>click</u>, <u>clack</u> and blow through if it's fuck me them bitch nigga fuck you. Bitch nigga what the fuck you gone do. With these fake motherfuckers I'm through. <u>Feeding</u> the <u>clip</u> my nigga just for you load up and release and watch the hollow flow through. You niggas know me and you know I don't know you but if it's fuck me than fuck you too. Kickback smoke a sac and do what I do. Tell your bitch to come through let it do what it do, I got potnas if you want them to slide through. Keep it real bitch I don't have any reason to lie to you I let you face reality now what the fuck you want wondo do. We can get down and dirty my niggas lets take it to the street. Throw up the dogs bitch nigga because it's time to eat. In times of war bitch nigga don't sleep. Eyes watching perparing for deep sleep. Why you hating on me bitch nigga when we all got to eat. Putting blunts in the air. It don't matter to me. We can peace up or let the guns bust. I don't give a fuck in these times of lust.

Keep it on the lap nigga fuck the trunk. Safety off cockback and dump with the nine mila mitter or that fully automatic pump bitch nigga I'm no punk. And that real. Sleeping with my little piece of pistal my bitch is so for real. We can keep the peace or cockback and unload and release the beast, shoot to kill what you hating ass niggas want to do I can be that nigga to click clack and blow through fuck me bitch nigga no fuck you what the fuck you gone do. No fuck you don't know about me but I know what hollows do spice it's fuck me bitch nigga I'll let the hollows fuck you

WHERE DID THE LOVE GO

JUSTICE IN LINE

BALANCE
HOW DOES ONE CHOOSE

Where did the love go. Can you tell me why doesn't the love show. Doing everything that a mans suppose too. Building one up just to make me fall. We were suppose to stick together so we won't fall. Instead I live in a world filled with fakeness and fanasy, trying to hold on to self. Staying as same as humanly possible. Doing what it takes to ease the pain of every day life. Living life and everyday paying the price. What's real to them may not be real to me. Searching for life hoping for a love to hold me. True to self and self kind. This love lost blows my mind. I play the game and the cards win every time. Doing what I have to do to ease my mind. I put a line out just in case some how I change my fate. Living a life that I appresheate. Where did my love go. Now that the love doesn't show.

On the search for realness. Letting the smoke flow

RE-LAX

RE-LAX
Getting mine
Regardless

$Regardless$
Dolla bill

(REWRITE POTENT)
FACE TO FACE

Bitch nigga you'd look <u>better in a boy</u> out here. Fucking with these nigga harder then crack rocks. With my nina next to me busting clips all day. Eyes out for these haters hating come always. Me and my chrome bitch loaded and ready for gun play. Nigga it's not up to me, you better listen to the gun spray. Loaded up and ready sitting on my black AK. No love for these bitch niggas with no love for me. Face to face fuck you I'm busting freely I'm standing in your face. Face to face with the with these nigga trying to take my place earse my face. Hating on your boy trying to take my face. We not related but I know the hollows tips can relate. Shaking the face off only kick it with the real, money motavated money makers shaking these haters off stacking on a mill with looks that can kill. But to me bitch nigga could better kissing steal you would look better in a box better yet. Filled up by the clip. Catching nothing but all shots. A bitch nigga wheater you like it or not, I'm out here loaded and ready to fill up your box. Bitch nigga move up for you get ready to catch shots to me bitch nigga you look better in the box fucking with these nigga harder than crack rocks.

<u>Stuck in rotation</u> watching the smoke bounce off the window. Don't know why I stay high watching the world fly bye and the smoke twist and turn as the blunts burn stuck in rotation waiting for my turn. Watching the sand in the hour glass drift away. Constantly rolling up blunts getting high all day, riding sky high watching the clouds pass in rotation as I puff puff pass. Staying high hoping to never come down grabing the blunt watching the smoke surround feeling the bass listening to the bass pound. Staying sky high when we fly high stuck on cloud nine trying to touch the sky, stuck in rotation as the blunts burn watching the smoke whirl waiting for my turn to fill my lungs with that sticky mean green with no stress finishing off this blunt while I'm waiting for the next blunt to come my way riding sky high getting high on the highway smoking that California lime, puffing purple crush watching the smoke swirl watching the clouds fly bye maintaining my high riding on the highway rolling sky high stuck in rotation wanting for the next blunt to fly bye. I love getting high so I can sit back and relax puff puff passing ready to twist another sac rolling up perfection yeah I know you love that staying sky high trying to touch the sky rolling up some end watch the clouds fly bye.

Stuck in rotation waiting for the next blunt to pass so high now I forgot to pass surrounded by weed smoke so potent and fire you rolled a good blunt but it not better then mine stuck in rotation chocking on lime think you can roll a better perfect to then here you go while I sit back relax and watch the smoke bounce off the window.

Nothing to do but to put weed on my mind breaking down a sac roll it up in no time. Smoking that <u>California lime</u> from that California line always about business. Keep that phone on at all times. Real G's don't fuck with the seeds, we break down pounds and smoke trees. Burning box after box. I don't give a fuck you don't smoke or not. Smelling like the essence of Mary Jane and I can't complaine. Sitting back relaxing take blunt, after blunt to the brain. Plam trees, bitches and bomb weed, all I need to stay keyned, smoking that purple cush untill my eye close shut, with a blunt in my mouth play boy I really don't give a fuck. Relaxed calm and collective you can take my bitch. But home boy you can't take this. Smoking that California lime with a California twist. Didn't think that you boy could smoke like this. Years of second guessing, stress, and depression, and it's my <u>THC</u> content they testing. While passing the blunt to me myself and eye. Why stay sobber when, I can stay high. Sit back relax and watchs the smoke clouds float bye. Doing my best to maintain. Roll up another blunt, and take it to the brain. To me smoking is my everyday thing. Blood shot eyes relaxing letting my nuts hang.

Riding through the block letting the chrome feet swang. So cool calm and collective putting my mind at ease. Kickback and relax and smoke these trees. Kickback relax and put my mind at ease. Riding down the highway engulfed by the trees. Never thought you could get so me much life from a seed. As I break down and roll up the rest of the weed. Back to the house to put my mind at ease, smoking pack after pack come get high with me. Buy a sac buy a pack come and fly with me. Get in where you fit in if you want to get high with me smoking pack after pack ain't no coming down for me.

JUMP, jump, how can you catch me slippin when I'm holding that my double barrel pump. Turned down the bass in the trunk. Just in case caught slippin I left some space in the trunk so don't go missing. Riding around the town with nina on my nuts sac nigga hate me because I'll bust back. Never affraid to bust, for funds we lust, and I'm getting mine even if I to cockback click clack goes the nine with a hole to the right side to ease your mind. Now bitch nigga what's with it. If you want it come and get it, nigga I ain't going nowhere I got two clips filled with hollow tips for you and boys can to share. Because I know niggas ain't got love for me nothing but mean mugs and fake hugs for me. Trust a fake nigga O no I'm not the one. I'm that nigga willing and ready holding this double barrel shoty to put holes in your body. Will I shoot these hating niggas for sho bitch niggas I'm all about that dough no love for these niggas catch me throwing hollows out the window buck shots through your rental for fucking with me. It fuck you bitch nigga for trying to fuck me. Cockback and unload and let the hollow flow. Bitch nigga don't fuck with me I'll let the bullets flow. Jump jump nigga and get hit by the pump dying of thrist. Bleeding from the twelve gauge bust.

<u>Bounce</u> from left to right keeping it moving when it's me and you, you know I ain't losing. That just me laying it on you like I was born to. Face down and ass out going deep with a fat blunt in my mouth. Never know what you got untill it's gone that's why I turn off my phone my attention is all your living in the moment of estacy with this beautyful bitch next to me. In the bedroom it's nothing except fucking around me making you moan coming all night yeah my game sex game tight. If you can keep me up baby we'll be up all night. Walking her to the bedroom when she feels like a fight. Don't matter pure darkness or the brightess light with you and me between the sheets, sweat dripping while we soak the sheets watching you look down to catch a peak. Loving how it feels when two meet. Staying up all night loving sounds when

AMERICAN DREAM

This shit is driving me insane. I'm a hustla and they knocking me. I'm the new hustla on the block and it ain't no stopping me. All these fake motherfuckers scheming and watching me. Living a hustlas life so they hating trying to stop me, watch me raise to the top, shake all these fake motherfucka scheming on my knot. Put a lid on your boy for hating on me for trying to make ends meet. I'm a hustla my nigga you know I got to eat living a hustlas life man it's hard on these streets. Dodging these hatras so they can't harrass me windows tinted so they roll right pass me. This shit driving me insane making money roll in stacks I'm holding money so tall my money stop folding. This hustlas life ain't peaches and cream trying to raise to the top to fulfill my American Dream. Mo money for show my nigga I'm all about the dough looking over my shoulder in case they try to take me out for show. Trying my best to relax with a fat blunt in my mouth. Man I telling these streets are nothing nice living the hard life and every day we roll the dice, and that's the life of a hustla.

Living a life with dope dealing dreams trying to reach the top by any and all means. I'm sorry I got to eat hustling trying my best to make ends meet. Just another day out here living on these mean streets, where playas play and hustlas grind just to eat, protecting my own with my chrome gripping my heat.

REWRITE
YEAH I MIGHT

<u>Yeah I might</u> grab the pistal's pistal grip load up and aim tight, homie I can load and unload all in the same night. Eyes of the dragon tiger never affraid to fight. Yeah I might slang yea all night to make ends meet and keep my grip tight these nigga can't see me. Yeah I might roll around town windows tinted windows rolled up letting the smoke fly round. Turn the bass volume up to increase the sound making the block feel me bust everytime I come around yeah I love that sound. Yeah I might let my nut hang riding around coasting letting my chrome feet swang, surrounded by smoke my everyday thing and yeah I might spit a flow slang CDs for show doing what I gotta do to roll in the dough I ain't a rapper but you can call me one for show. Yeah I might let yo chick harrass my <u>DICK</u>, shaven nut sac now bitch lick, I'm so sick. Yeah I might get hand cuffed and arrested harrassed and tested. Homie I'm raising to the top now no second guessing if hustling is the problem then money is the answer. Time to stack using everything I've learn with and to burn action and progress more money less problems speed bumbs in the way, let the money solve them.

And yeah I might down bottles after bottles fuck model after model jump in the ride and smash the model and I'm gone with a pack a blunts to the face as I roll on stuffing my face music blasting. Yeah I might get my drink on. Take shots of protrone Bacardi one fifty one untill I'm done no need for a ride I'm with family son. Shot parties keep the gen on the run I do this for money the loot family. Bitches and for fun always got my nina docked in case somebody wants some. And yeah I might put them beer gagols on when it's nothing else to do I gets my fuck on homeboy I thought you know and yeah I might!!!!! Ect.

Stay up all night get to crush growing can't you see me moving on the nose drip up all night. Fuck you yeah I might I don't give a fuck as long as my money is wouned tight pistol grip loaded ready to produce like dynmite. And yeah I might stay out of sight when the law rolls in they might hold me for 24 <u>twenty four</u> and I'll be out buy ten and yeah I might

• Common ground and/or creatures (people do what they want to do people do what they can do)

• <u>Women</u> are like a rotating equations. The answer is always different, depending on their mood/and or situation.

I
(this will help find the answer)
[I = idea
W = want
WWG or A = what was <u>gotten</u> or/and <u>gained</u>] ((theory) <u>idea)</u>
Gained (<u>Action</u>)
(I + W) = WWG or (W + I) = A (Feeling what someone needs. <u>Bonding</u>)
the ((a need) <u>want</u>)
<u>varible</u> that always changing
<u>variable</u> keep changing
<u>almost</u> ∞ <u>Never</u> the same
(what was gotten)
•How can one solve for a answer when the problem keep changing?
* (One must <u>find what is wanted</u>)
• Must live life to solve. Everyday, every <u>time</u> is a different answer.
• Must rotate allong side. Hope you figured out the answer.

Object moves through space at high speed faster than light speed of to slow time down and reverse it, find out at what speed <u>can</u> this happen,? and how to make it happen?

II
• Object cutting through time, and space. Creating some kind of <u>loop</u> with in space moving, building up speed, untill the object, and time start to reverse
(• It's a <u>fact</u> that time slows down after passing the <u>speed of light</u>. Proven by NASA.
• (One must be careful when dealing with the past so one doesn't change self.)
past make the future
<u>past</u> + <u>present</u> = <u>future</u>
• or may <u>vica versa</u>

H being = time
(How to become part of time is the answer to eternal life.)

I picked this collection of songs and poems to inspire the world with my expression and view of life from my point of view. I started writing these pieces of art many years ago when I was surrounded by hater in a great time of need. I had to take a journey inside myself and create my own happiness and these songs, poems, and information poured out through a pen, helping me in a great time of need. I wanted to share with you the reader this collection of ideas, hoping to entertain and tickle the imagination of the world. The creation of this collection was a great step in the right direction in a great time of need. I am pleased with the outcome of this collection and hope to bring greater understanding peace, love, happiness and entertainment to you the reader in this great journey called life.

Printed in the United States
By Bookmasters